A Bias for Murder

Books by Sally Goldenbaum

Queen Bees Quilt Shop Mysteries:

A Patchwork of Clues
A Thread of Darkness
A Bias for Murder

Seaside Knitters Society Mysteries:

Murder Wears Mittens
How to Knit a Murder

A Bias for Murder

Sally Goldenbaum

LYRICAL UNDERGROUND
Kensington Publishing Corp.
www.kensingtonbooks.com

LYRICAL UNDERGROUND BOOKS are published by

Kensington Publishing Corp.
119 West 40th Street
New York, NY 10018

All Kensington titles, imprints, and distributed lines are available at special quantity discounts for bulk purchases for sales promotion, premiums, fund-raising, educational, or institutional use.

Special book excerpts or customized printings can also be created to fit specific needs. For details, write or phone the office of the Kensington Sales Manager: Kensington Publishing Corp., 119 West 40th Street, New York, NY 10018. Attn. Sales Department. Phone: 1-800-221-2647.

Lyrical Underground and Lyrical Underground logo Reg. US Pat. & TM Off.

First Electronic Edition: August 2019
ISBN-13: 978-1-5161-0909-8 (ebook)
ISBN-10: 1-5161-0909-0 (ebook)

First Print Edition: August 2019
ISBN-13: 978-1-5161-0910-4
ISBN-10: 1-5161-0910-4

Printed in the United States of America

The Crestwood Quilters

Portia (Po) Paltrow: Writer of quilting articles and books

Phoebe Mellon: Mother of toddler twins

Kate Simpson: Part-time graduate student and substitute teacher

Eleanor Canterbury: Octogenarian and heir to the Canterbury family fortune

Leah Sarandon: Professor of women's studies at Canterbury College

Selma Parker: Owner of Parker's Dry Goods Store

Maggie Helmers: Crestwood veterinarian

Susan Miller: Shop manager

Prelude

Oliver Harrington walked down the back staircase from his second-floor bedroom, one hand gripping the banister tightly.

The noises had come from the kitchen right below his bedroom. A shuffling sound. A strange cat, maybe. Some smug feline finding Neptune's cat door in the basement and making its way up for food.

He wasn't afraid of the noise, not really. Things made him anxious sometimes, but not afraid. In fact, Ollie couldn't remember ever being afraid in all his fifty-two years. He didn't get angry much, either. Hardly ever. But he was angry this time, angrier than he had ever been in his whole life. Because it wasn't fair. None of it. That's probably why he was hearing things. It wasn't a cat after all. It was the uncomfortable rumblings of anger rattling around in his head.

Narrow windows along the old staircase looked out over the lawns and gardens of the Harrington Estate. But Oliver's eyes didn't see the lawns and gardens; Ollie looked up, as he always did, up toward the magnificent galaxy spread like a gauzy quilt above the town, above his house. So magnificent it took his breath away.

A deep, starry night. Ollie could see the great Andromeda Galaxy with his naked eye. He paused on the staircase, his breath catching in his throat. Exquisite. Miraculous. Nearly three million light-years away, and he could see it from this window of his home in small Crestwood, Kansas. It was surely a miracle. How could people not see that? How could they not revel in its mystery? But some did. Ollie did.

Finally, forcing himself to breathe, as if the dazzling beauty of the universe above him was almost more than he could handle, Ollie took another step down. For as long as he could remember, this was where he found peace—looking up into the universe, relishing the knowledge of how it all worked. Bowing to its majesty and mystery. The amazement never dimmed, just like the North Star.

"Glorious," he said, the single word traveling out of his mouth and piercing the still, predawn air, echoing down the hardwood stairs before him.

When Oliver was a boy, the back staircase had been the way servants got to the kitchen quickly and silently from their third-floor rooms. He couldn't remember when that had changed. Probably when he and his twin sister were college age and Adele went off to her East Coast school, but he couldn't be sure.

Oliver had lived in the Harrington mansion nearly his whole life. He'd left briefly for a junior college in the east, a school his mother chose carefully, one that would offer extra attention to her special son, and give him a chance to explore the things he loved—astronomy, writing.

It hadn't worked. They made him take other subjects that didn't capture his mind and spirit, and Oliver failed. And years later, he finally got the degree that would have pleased his mother, a bachelor's in science from Canterbury College. Or university, as they wanted to call it now, though it seemed a little uppity to Ollie. And then the professors had let him stay on, taking any classes he wanted to take. And even most Crestwood students treated him like a person, not someone they considered odd because he didn't talk about sports and dancing and girlfriends.

A bang beneath him halted Oliver's movement and he stood still on the bottom step. It wasn't soft like his cat.

But it was alive.

Probably some neighborhood kid playing a trick on me. Maybe he should start locking his doors. His friend Halley had been surprised when she discovered he didn't lock up. But she didn't grow up in a small town—she didn't understand. *Halley worried about too many things,* he thought, his will and deeds and things that didn't matter much to Oliver. Other people worried about those things, too, but Ollie just smiled and agreed, and that seemed to make everyone feel better.

His brown eyes fought the fog of darkness in front of him. Finally, his bare feet felt the flat surface of the kitchen floor and he slid one hand across the wall, his fingers finding the light switch. He flicked it on.

Yellow light fell on the wide-planked flooring and bounced off the stainless steel counter and refrigerator. The kitchen was big enough to feed an army, Halley had told him the other day, but Oliver kept every surface clean and sparkling. He loved the stainless tops because you could see the perfect reflection of the entire room, even his own face. Sometimes he saw Halley's in it, too, standing there beside him. Oliver loved the orderliness of the kitchen, the pots hanging in order of size, the cups in the glass-fronted cabinets lined up in perfect symmetry. He loved this house. His home. His memories.

It was way too big for him, he knew that, and all sorts of people were telling him that these days. *Move to a condo, Ollie,* Tom Adler kept telling him. *I'll find you the best in the city and take this monster off your hands.*

But 210 Kingfish Drive wasn't a monster at all. It was home. Always would be.

Ollie looked around the room and out the window to the wooded backyard, back toward the pond that Joe, his gardener, tended to. No branches moved in the Indian summer night. No sound. Only the silence of the stars. Silly. No one was here. Just in his dreams, that's all.

Oliver pressed the boiling water button on his sink and filled a china cup, then scooped up a cup of loose herbed tea from the canister on the counter. He and Halley and Joe had laughed about that the other day— how Ollie made midnight trips to the kitchen for a cup of tea. They didn't believe him that herbed tea solved all ills. But it was true. He'd sleep like a baby. A cup of ginger tea and the fog in his head would clear. It would scatter his silly thoughts of a strange kitty cat coming into his house to visit Neptune or steal a bit of food.

He leaned against the counter, his bare feet planted on the smooth wooden floor, and slowly sipped his tea. The room brought him comfort and he could almost smell the chicken noodle soup the cook used to make for him when he was sick, the hot biscuits she would bring all the way up to his room. The back door led out to a small enclosed porch where years ago the milkman left bottles of fresh milk and where the Harrington twins would line up their boots after building snowmen in the backyard.

The door to the porch was slightly ajar. Oliver frowned. Had he left it open when he let his cat back in the house before going to bed? He walked over and closed it with the flat of his hand, then jumped at the noise. And then the meow. Through a window in the door, he spotted a small cat on the porch, staring up at him with accusing eyes. "Neptune," he said. The word came out on a sigh of relief. Ollie smiled and let the black cat in. Mystery solved. That's what he'd heard, his sweet Neptune.

Oliver sipped his tea, staring out into the starry night, knowing he needed sleep and strength for what the new day would bring. He hated confrontations, but he couldn't let it go this time. It was wrong. Plain and simple. Against the law.

Sally Goldenbaum

He drained the last liquid from the cup and rested back against the counter again, the cold edge pressing through his thin bathrobe. Time to go back upstairs, read that little collection of Loren Eiseley's essays that Halley had given him. Fall asleep with visions of galaxies filling his head. And he'd deal with tomorrow, tomorrow.

Oliver left his mother's Limoges teacup in the sink and headed for the stairs. The tea had done its magic and a dreamy fog settled over him. He pulled himself up the first step, then another. Sleep. It was on its way.

Oliver reached the first landing where the steps curved back upon themselves and a small window lighted his path. He paused for a minute, taking in a breath of air, then frowned as the brightness of the stars beyond the window dimmed.

An eclipse? No, it wasn't time. He squinted at the window, moving now, in and out, wide and narrow, like a fun house mirror. The tree branches beyond, leaves falling. Humming, dancing in slow motion.

Ollie released his hold of the walnut railing. A dance. He was dancing, moving slowly through the air. A ghost in the night.

Neptune stood at the foot of the stairs, her green eyes watching as Oliver's long slender body turned slightly, then bent at the waist, doubled over, and slowly somersaulted down to the wide-planked kitchen floor.

Neptune meowed, then walked over to Oliver's face and gently licked his moist sharp chin with her gravely tongue.

Chapter 1

News of Ollie Harrington's death caused a ripple of sadness through the Canterbury University community and the neighborhood where his family had lived for generations.

But a larger ripple—nearly a tidal wave, Po Paltrow thought—occurred almost immediately after when Ollie's twin sister, Adele, elegant and self-assured, swept down upon the small town of Crestwood a day Ollie Harrington died.

Shades of Isadora Duncan, Po thought that day when she spotted Adele Harrington speeding down Elderberry Road in her long elegant Cadillac convertible, a yellow scarf tied around her neck and flying in the autumn breeze. *A veritable whirlwind.* But the thought that Adele's arrival would cause a chaos of rather momentous proportions—at least for Crestwood Kansas—was beyond Po's imagination. Not then. Not when people were still able to conjure up sympathy for a grieving woman who had lost her twin brother.

Adele's years away had made her an unfamiliar figure to most residents, but in the space of two days she had quickly and efficiently taken over the Harrington mansion, disturbed quiet neighbors with strident demands to trim trees and keep children away from her property, and alienated nearly everyone else in town, including the family's lawyers and especially the police.

Even the group gathering in Selma Parker's quilt shop on Elderberry Road was affected by the woman who had come to bury her brother.

"Like who would have imagined a quiet man like Oliver Harrington would have a sister like *that!*" said Phoebe Mellon, the youngest member of the group, as she looked around the cluttered table, searching for a pair of scissors.

Eleanor Canterbury handed them to Phoebe. "It's a shame. Adele may have come back to bury her brother, but she's doing damage to the Harrington name with her demands and rude manners." A rare note of displeasure crept into the lively voice of the Quilters' only octogenarian. Eleanor picked up a square of flowered red fabric and examined it through her bifocals to see if she had left any stray threads hanging. Doing all her piecing by hand—mostly because it was portable that way and she could take it with her to Paris or New Guinea or wherever she might be headed—was tedious but practical, and as Eleanor herself said in her perfectly gracious voice, "I am damn good at it." The crazy quilt table runner she was finishing bore testimony to her words.

"But you have to admit that she's adding some excitement, El," Phoebe said. "Even moms in my twins' playgroup are gabbing about her. Word has it she eats three-year-olds."

Po laughed at Phoebe's irreverent comment, the kind they'd come to expect from her. She looked to the end of the table at Selma Parker. "Selma, what do you think is up with Adele? I remember her, certainly, but mostly from events when she'd come back to town to visit family. Did you know her?"

"I knew her mother," Selma said. She wet one finger, then touched the iron to be sure it was hot. The Saturday quilt group had met in the back of Selma's fabric store for as long as anyone could remember, beginning back when Selma's mother ran the shop. Members changed as life ran its course, daughters and granddaughters and sometimes friends of original members taking their place. And Selma loved it all—especially the present group, an unlikely mixture of women with an age span of nearly sixty years, anchored on either end by Phoebe and Eleanor. Though the group had begun as quilting companions, their lives had become as intricately entwined as the strips of fabric they deftly fashioned into works of art.

Satisfied that the iron was hot and the sewing machine was ready to go, Selma looked back at Po. "Adele didn't stick around Crestwood long, as you probably remember. She came back for a short while after graduating from Smith College. But she couldn't settle down. I remembered her own mother urging her to go back east. Encouraging her to leave. She told her that Crestwood wasn't big enough for her. There seemed to be some tension in the family, but it was never talked about, of course. Walter Harrington was a pompous, arrogant, man—"

"Aha," Maggie Helmers interrupted, "it's in the genes, then."

"Well, Ollie sure didn't inherit them. He was a very lovely man. Simple, but at the same time, oh-so-smart," Po said. "He would sometimes walk by our house when Scott and I were out in the yard, and he'd walk up the drive, telling Scott about something he had learned in science class, talking quickly and continuously about whatever it was that had captivated him. I think he figured that as president of Canterbury College, Scott would know everything."

"That's really sweet," Kate Simpson said. "I kind of remember that, although I was nothing but a squirt when Ollie hung around."

"I'm sure he seemed a little different to you kids, Po said. "I don't think he fit in with his peers as much as with adults."

"Well, it's no surprise he stopped at your house, Po," Maggie said. "People like you and Scott would make anyone feel comfortable. People, cats, dogs, hermit crabs."

Po laughed. "Well, I think Ollie made a place for himself here in Crestwood."

"But not his sister. I remember Adele not liking Crestwood much, especially once she got a taste of the East Coast." Eleanor said.

"Apparently that hasn't changed," Kate said. She pushed her chair back from the table and took a drink of coffee, trying hard not to spill it on the mounds of fat quarters piled on the table. "The neighborhood kids are already calling her the wicked witch of the north. But I feel kind of sorry for her. This can't be easy for her, coming back to bury her twin brother. Maybe this is how she handles grief, keeping people at arms' length on purpose. She's probably not so bad." Kate had come back to Crestwood to bury her own mother several years before, and the memory was still fresh, though cushioned now as sweet memories filled in around her loss.

"Bad? Kate, she's downright nasty," Maggie said. "She brought her dog into my clinic yesterday. The waiting room was packed because Daisy Bruin's beagle was hit by a car. He's fine now. But anyway, Adele elbowed her way to the counter and demanded that Emerson be seen immediately. She was so rude. And then—" Maggie's hands gestured while she talked, and she waved several pieces of freezer paper onto the floor. "And then when Mandy—my new technician—tried to calm her down and explain why she'd have to wait, Adele told her she had bad breath and should see a dentist."

Po shook her head. No matter how badly Adele was acting, her grief was still fresh. She picked up a finished block of her quilt hanging and held it up to the light to check the hand stitching on the abstract design. She was trying something new—piecing together bright oranges and yellows and minty green strips in wavy swooshes. *She would put it in the upper hallway*, she thought, where it would brighten up the interior space. "I agree with Kate. Imagine all that she's dealing with. Figuring out the service, the burial, and what to do with that enormous house. It's difficult—"

"So you haven't heard?" Leah asked, her brows lifting in surprise.

"What?" Maggie, Phoebe, and Kate asked in unison.

"People at the university went over as soon as Adele arrived. Professor Fellers suggested the college help with the memorial service for Oliver. Jed Fellers was Ollie's mentor, you know, and he spent a lot of time with him. Ollie was such a sweet guy—a little different like you said, Po—but he loved the library and learning and the college. He even sat in on some of my classes once in a while. Anyway, Adele said no to Jed's offer."

"Why?" Po asked. "That was such a generous offer. And appropriate. The college was Ollie's world. That and the galaxy."

Leah took a breath, then filled in the rest of the story. "Her brother's body was already gone when she arrived."

"Gone where?" Phoebe asked.

"Probably to the funeral home," Maggie said. "If Adele came in a day later, maybe whoever takes care of their estate matters had the body removed."

"No," Leah said. "It was gone because the police had it moved to the morgue and are arranging for an autopsy."

"What?" Eleanor asked. "Why? He had a heart attack, right?"

"But Ollie was in great health. And sometimes in cases like that, an autopsy is done—even though it's entirely possible he did die of a heart attack. Apparently, whoever made the decision was new to the police department and thought Ollie had no family, so no one got Adele's permission to move the body. She was furious about the whole thing, the way it was handled. Everything. Perhaps that's why she's been less than civil to people."

"I'm not sure I blame her," Po said. "Having your twin die unexpectedly is an awful thing. But they can still help her plan a memorial. It will just be slightly delayed."

Leah shook her head. "According to university officials, she doesn't want anything. No memorial. No funeral. Ollie will be cremated as soon as they allow her to arrange it."

The group fell silent, massaging the news by concentrating on the beautiful pieces of material in front of them. The cotton squares of color, vibrant enough to light up a dreary day.

"Do you suppose Adele will leave soon, then?" Phoebe asked. "What will happen to the home on Kingfish Drive? My in-laws say it's worth zillions."

"It's a magnificent home," Po said. "I remember going to parties there when Adele and Oliver's parents were alive. And I stopped by now and then when I saw Ollie around, just to say hello, to take him some cobbler or bread. He'd always been a bit of a loner, but we had good talks. I was fond of him."

"Did you know that the house is haunted?" Phoebe asked. "Shelly Rampey at my kids' playgroup told us all about it. But that can be, like, good, depending on the ghosts, I guess. Shelly said that her yoga teacher is wanting to buy the place for a retreat house for busy moms—a place they can go to refresh their spirits. I said, 'sign me up, sister.'"

"Phoebe, if your spirit were any more refreshed, we'd have to tie you down," Po said.

Phoebe giggled.

"I wish you'd been alive to watch Goldie Hawn on an old TV show, *Laugh In,*" Eleanor said as she laughed right along with Phoebe's contagious sound. "You laugh just like her. And even look a little bit the same."

Po laughed too, agreeing wholeheartedly. "But about that property— Phoebe's in-laws are right. It's priceless. Neighbors are already concerned that it might be sold to the wrong party."

"What's that mean?" Kate asked. She reached behind her and grabbed a pastry from the side table.

"Well, it's almost too big for a single family, at least nowadays. And the neighbors don't want anything that will bring traffic, that sort of thing. That's understandable. And there are so many beautiful old magnolias and oaks and pines on that property—the thought of a developer tearing it down and putting up condos is very sad. I think it's one of the oldest houses in Crestwood. It needs to be taken care of properly."

"Do you think Adele Harrington will care about any of that?" Eleanor asked, her tone of voice conveying her own opinion clearly.

"The house has been in the family for over one hundred years. Adele will surely consider that and do the right thing." But Po frowned as she spoke. The "right thing" was a very relative term in cases like this.

"Well, the controversy surrounding that beautiful old home is waking up a sleepy Crestwood," Eleanor said.

"That's for sure," Kate said. "I ran by it this morning and there's all sorts of activity going on—cars, a couple trucks, people walking around the front taking pictures. It was crazy and noisy. I wondered why the neighbors weren't out protesting it all."

Eleanor had driven by too. "I noticed Tom Adler's Prairie Development truck moving like a drunk snail past the place."

"He's been after 210 Kingfish Drive for years," Po said.

"And I'm not sure I share your confidence in Adele's sense of doing what's right, Po," Selma said. "She doesn't live here, after all, and doesn't give a hoot about the town." Selma sat with her back to the main room of the store, one ear on the customers being helped by two college girls who helped out on Saturdays. "There's so much money at stake. If you ask me, that's what will decide what happens to that beautiful home—money. Mark my words. And let's just hope it helps the town, not hurts it."

"Why, Selma Parker," a new voice floated into the mix. "Who would ever dream of hurting this little town?" Heads moved in unison and all eyes focused on the tall, commanding figure standing in the wide doorway, directly behind Selma.

The woman smiled slightly, acknowledging them as a group. Then her gray eyes focused on Selma, and she took a step into the room. "Please, don't let me interrupt, ladies. Go on with your chitchat. I find your conversation quite amusing."

Selma stood and wiped the palms of her sweaty hands down her rumpled slacks. Then she held one hand out in greeting and forced a smile. "Hello, Adele," she said. "It's been a long time."

Chapter 2

Adele Harrington brushed pastry crumbs off the table and set down her Balenciaga bag.

"Yes, it has, Selma." Adele turned her angular face toward Po. "And Portia Paltrow, you've aged agreeably, I see."

Po felt the tension in the room but forced a smile to her face. "We're all sad to hear about your brother, Adele. He will be missed."

Adele waved her long fingers through the air as if dismissing Po's thought. "Death happens. Perhaps Oliver would have lived longer if he hadn't shut himself up in that house like a damn monk. He was a genius, you know." Adele looked around the table. She looked at Phoebe for a long time and finally shook her head. "Who are you, young lady? And what did you do to your hair?"

Phoebe waved away the reprimand. "My name is Phoebe Mellon."

"Mellon?" Adele said. Her voice indicated she was about to argue with Phoebe about her name.

"Yes. *Those* Mellons. You might know them. I'm married to their son."

Adele frowned, as if unable to accept that a woman with a pixie haircut could be a part of a notable Crestwood family.

Phoebe raked her fingers through her shorn hair, which she had clipped down to an inch or two once Jude and Emma were born. "It's not exactly a debutante cut but it sure helps when you have twin toddlers." Her tone was just like her pixie haircut—friendly and happy.

Adele's hand had risen to her shoulder-length hair, smoothing it as she stared at Phoebe's head. "So you're married to that Mellon boy," she said, as if those were the last words she had heard.

"Is there something you wanted, Adele?" Selma asked, dismissing the moment and hoping Phoebe wouldn't run for her FlowBee haircutting device and offer to cut Adele's hair too. Phoebe wouldn't allow herself to be pushed around for too long. "Would you like a cup of coffee? There's a plate of Marla's pastries over on the side table. These must be difficult days for you."

Adele was silent for a moment, as if considering the coffee question, then she looked over at Phoebe again. "I like your spunk. It will fare you well with that family."

She turned back to Selma, her face softer. "And yes, I'd like a cup of coffee."

Po wondered what Adele had done in her years away from Crestwood. Offering opinions certainly came easily to her. She poured a cup of coffee and handed it to her. "Cream and sugar are on the table."

Adele nodded her thanks and sat down next to Po. "I'd like to talk with all of you."

A befuddled look passed among the women at the table as they fiddled with needles and pieces of fabric.

Selma touched the iron to see if it was hot. "This is a quilting group, Adele. You're welcome to stay, but we'll want to continue finishing up our—"

"I know what this is, Selma. My mother was a member of this group, lest you forget."

Eleanor smiled from her corner chair, remembering. "Of course she was. Dolores Harrington was an excellent quilter and a very lovely woman."

Po watched Eleanor's face and held back a smile, reading her friend's thought. *And how in the world did she bear the likes of you?* But Eleanor, thankfully, held her silence.

Adele looked over, noticing the elegant gray-haired woman for the first time. "Eleanor Canterbury?" she said. "Good grief, are you still alive?"

Eleanor's delicious laughter floated above the cluttered table. "I suppose that's a matter of opinion, Adele. But yes, I believe I am. Would you like a pinch?" She held out her arm. Dangly gold bracelets chimed against one another.

Adele stared at Eleanor for a moment. "Amazing." She shook her head. "My mother liked you, if I remember correctly."

"Your mother liked everyone, Adele," Eleanor said. "And everyone liked her."

"You're right about that, Eleanor." Adele smiled for the first time. "Please go on with your work, but I'd like to tell you why I'm here."

"That would be nice," Selma said. She picked up an all-white hanging that she had made for a new stationery store opening up down the road, looking down at the feather pen and scrolled piece of paper design if it might hold some words of wisdom in response to whatever Adele had to say.

"How cool is that, Selma!" Phoebe said. She leaned over the shop owner's shoulder and touched the stitching with the tip of her finger. "That's perfect for the stationery store!"

Adele cleared her throat, pulling attention back to her.

"Adele, do you know everyone here?" Po asked. "We sometimes get so involved in our art that we forget there is a world beyond it."

"I can see that you do." Adele glanced around the table. "I know who most of you are. I've checked the group out."

Po frowned. Checked them out? What on earth was Adele Harrington thinking, coming in and confronting them this way? Her brother's death had been a shock. That had to be the explanation.

"You're Kate Simpson," Adele said, looking at Kate. Her tone was accusatory, as if she were making some sort of judgment.

Po looked over at her goddaughter. Even in jeans and a T-shirt, her normal Saturday attire, Kate stood out in a crowd, not always for reasons that pleased her mother or her mother's best friend. But that morning Kate had been unusually silent, her too-loud laugh absent. But she was still Kate and still stood out in a crowd. She was the tallest of the quilters by several inches, as slender as Kansas wheat, and her thick, unruly hair seemed to have a life of its own. Kate leveled a look at Adele, as if wondering what Adele would do if she denied Adele's declaration.

To Po's relief, she didn't.

"I am," Kate said simply.

The two women must have met several times, Po thought, although she wasn't sure if Adele remembered. The Simpson's house was just a couple blocks from the Harrington mansion, and Adele knew Kate's mother, of course.

"I've seen you riding that fool bike past the house," Adele said. Then, abruptly, she turned her attention to Maggie and nodded, recognition and a trace of pleasure softening the sculpted lines of her face. "I've met you, Dr. Helmers," she said. "You are good to my Emerson."

Maggie nodded. "Emerson is a wonderful dog."

"Yes, he is." Adele managed a smile, enough to ease the tension that was settling around the table. "Dogs are a great comfort."

Leah Sarandon fiddled with a pair of scissors sitting in front of her. She had been watching Adele carefully, wondering if she would recognize her.

"And you are?" Adele asked now. "You don't appear to be a Crestwood native."

She didn't remember, Leah thought, which was fine. "I'm from the East Coast, but my husband and I have lived here for a while. I teach at Canterbury and my husband is a pediatrician in town."

"And you do some of the design work with this group?"

"Some. I like to try new things with the group and they indulge me."

Adele nodded, as if in some sort of approval. "And yes, I do remember you. You attended the college banquet honoring my brother several years ago. I never forget a face, although your name escaped me."

Adele seemed to study Leah for a moment and then she said, "You were on the committee that chose his essay on the Milky Way over the other submissions. It was unusual attention given to a nontraditional student, something of which you can be proud."

They were all looking at Adele now, her voice several decibels quieter as she spoke about her brother.

"HIs essay was sparse and elegant," Leah said.

"It was that. As his professor said, 'it was the work of a genius.'"

Leah agreed. "Jed Fellers is head of the astronomy department and he considered Ollie his protégé. He took your brother under his wing and encouraged him to write, to learn. He made Ollie feel at home at the college."

"As well he should have," Adele said.

Her sentence was definite, ending the conversation. Her gaze moved on and rested on Susan Miller, sitting next to Leah.

Before Adele could ask, the shop assistant introduced herself, and told Adele that when she wasn't working with Selma, she, too, was a nontraditional student, thanks to her generous employer, who had insisted she return to school to get her fiber arts degree.

"It was pure selfishness," Selma said with a laugh. "What Susan has learned about design and fibers has benefited all of us. And all my customers, too."

"Are you responsible for that quilt display in the college library?" Adele asked.

"Leah and I put that together," Susan said. "They often display students' work. Recently they have featured quilts honoring life on the Kansas prairie, all designed and quilted by Kansas women."

"It's a fine display," Adele said. "I never liked the Kansas prairie. Too barren for me. But seeing it on those quilts made me see it differently."

The sudden compliment from the unlikely source caused Po to chuckle. "Adele Harrington, I believe you are all show," she said. "But we still don't know why you're here with us. I know you must have a million things on your plate."

"Po's right," Selma said. "I'm sure getting that huge house of yours ready for an eager market is a formidable task."

"An eager market?" Adele frowned.

"I'd say that everyone from the college board of directors to the city council to outside investors would like nothing better than to be the proud owners of your beautiful acreage and that amazing house." Po took a sip of coffee.

"Is that what this silly town thinks?"

Po frowned at the curious comment, but she wasn't inclined to ask for an explanation. Instead, she continued in her own direction. "Those of us who love old beautiful estates are hopeful you'll be discriminating when you decide who will own it next. Large condos wouldn't endear you to the neighbors." Po chose her words carefully. She had no right to tell Adele what to do with her inheritance, even if she could. Although she'd love for the house to be preserved, she wasn't sure what the best choice would be. Perhaps a small museum to house local art? Something that wouldn't cause traffic jams, something tasteful and discrete.

"And do you think I care about being liked by the neighbors, Po?" Adele asked.

"Yes," Po said. There was something forced about Adele's attitude. Po remembered her as a young woman, home from her first year at Smith. She had come over to the house one day with her mother. Po and Scott had recently moved into the home she still lived in. Po remembered it with some clarity because while Adele's mother and Scott talked about a donation the Harringtons wanted to give to the college, Adele talked with her, excited about the things she was learning and the thrill of living near Boston and soaking up all it had to offer. Po wasn't that far removed from her own experience at Radcliffe, and they had shared stories about classes and clubs and what are called the Seven Sister schools.

Adele had seemed older than her years even then, but her enthusiasm for life and learning had been obvious. This austere facade she had adopted in her fifties didn't seem a totally comfortable fit, and Po wondered if grief and loss had hardened her.

Selma looked around the table, then asked again "You mentioned you need to talk with us about something. How can we help? Is it with a service, a memorial for Ollie?"

"Of course not. I will handle anything that pertains to Ollie." She sighed, as if her patience was being tried. She looked around the table, at each of the women, then the pieces of fabric in front of them.

Confused, the women went back to work, their fingers the only movement in the room.

Finally, Adele placed the palms of her hands on the table as if addressing a jury. "I'm here on business. I want to hire you to make eight quilts for me."

Eight sets of fingers ceased movement.

"Immediately," Adele added.

"What are you talking about?" Selma said. She put down her fabric and looked over the top of her glasses.

"You heard me, Selma Parker. I want you to make eight quilts for me. I will pay you whatever you require, of course—I don't ask for favors. You can donate it to that quilt museum I hear you want to start, or whatever." Her long thin fingers waved the air. "I will even donate extra to the cause. I want beautiful pieced quilt tops—I have already made arrangements to have them quilted as soon as you finish piecing them. I would like you to begin working on them right away."

"Why in heaven's name do you want eight quilts?" Selma asked.

"I want twelve quilts. But my mother preserved some of her own, and I'll use four of those."

"Use them for what?" Kate asked.

"For 210 Kingfish Road—my elegant new bed and breakfast."

Chapter 3

The news that Adele Harrington was turning the Harrington mansion into a B&B hit Crestwood with the force of a Kansas tornado.

The issue wasn't that the idea was foreign to residents—Crestwood was the perfect place for a cozy B&B. The town already boasted two small inns near the Emerald River. Parents of Canterbury students kept them full and profitable.

It was other things, especially the fact that the Harrington property was probably the most valuable private home in the entire town, and many had an eye on it for far loftier enterprises than a cozy place for folks to spend the night and wake up to omelets and homemade cinnamon rolls.

And then there were the neighborhood concerns. The well-heeled residents who coveted privacy and quiet. Po had already heard the concern in neighbors' voices.

"There'll be traffic messes, ungodly noise—and they'll probably start having weddings and God knows what over there," a nearby neighbor had bellowed.

But Po knew it was even more than that. It was the change in the quiet, tree-canopied Crestwood area that they feared. A B&B this year, and what would be next? It was the loss of control over what happened to their neighborhood and what might possibly precipitate a dip in property values. It was *change*, something longtime residents feared.

And then there were those who missed Ollie Harrington. Who liked the middle-aged man who fed birds and looked at stars and never, ever called the police when neighborhood children climbed his trees or tried to fish in his pond. These were the people who couldn't imagine a woman planning on disrupting her brother's home before his body was even laid to rest. What kind of woman would do that?

An awful one, they suspected.

But the remaining Harrington heir had bested them all, making any protests irrelevant. She had instantly found loopholes in the zoning laws for a home that had graced the land before most of Crestwood even existed. It was going to be a bed and breakfast.

And there was nothing anyone in all of Crestwood could do about it.

* * * *

"People are so furious that I'm almost ashamed we're making these quilts for her," Kate said as she and Po wandered about the city market late that morning. "On the other hand, it's an interesting project."

Once Adele had left the shop, ideas for the Harrington quilts began bouncing off the walls. In the end, they'd decided to focus on traditional patterns for most of the inn's rooms, using old patterns from the *Kansas City Star* newspaper collection. The familiar patterns would be perfect for Adele's bed and breakfast, they'd all agreed. Picking eight from the thousands that had been published would be the hard part.

"It'll be a challenge. But I agree. It'll be fun." Po stopped at an apple booth and felt the Granny Smith apples, wondering aloud if they'd be good for a pie.

Though summer squash had given way to pumpkins and apples, the market was still buzzing with activity. Situated on the banks of the Emerald River, the open-air market was part of a cleaned-up area that had given rise in recent years to a park and several small restaurants on the edge of the downtown area. Run by farmers and residents who brought in organic produce and herbs and flowers from May to late September, the market was a vibrant place for visitors and townsfolk to gather on sunny Saturday mornings. The smell of fritters and hot coffee filled the air, and local musicians played in the small white gazebo while children danced on its steps and old folks filled the benches and clapped their hands to the music.

Po picked up a jar of pesto and read the hand-lettered label. "But Adele's decision is certainly causing a fuss," she said, and filled Kate in on the neighborhood meeting. "A friend of mine in the neighborhood invited me along and it was clear that this isn't making Adele any friends."

"Do you think Adele Harrington cares a whit about friends?" Kate asked.

"Point well taken." Po handed Kate an apple from her bag.

"You don't have to tell me what you're talking about." Leah walked over from a nearby pumpkin stand. Her denim skirt swept her ankles and a chunky necklace moved on her hand-screened T-shirt. She twisted a bead as she talked. "Did you read any news last night or today? Who would have thought one individual could create such a stir?"

"I thought a lot about it last night and, well, really, there are a lot worse things that could be done with that property," Po said. "There will be twelve bedrooms, that's maybe a maximum of twenty-five people plus staff. Not exactly a traffic jam, especially with that long driveway and all the space beside the house and beyond. And there are enough trees shielding the estate that most neighbors won't even notice."

"Maybe it's the idea that Adele is going to be living there that's infuriating people," Kate said. "She isn't exactly a warm and welcoming innkeeper type."

Po laughed. "Maybe. But frankly I think it's the other disappointed parties that are causing the furor. The neighbors will adjust. Some of them simply want to hear their own voices. It's the people who wanted the property for monetary interests who are encouraging the protests."

"I can vouch for the college's disappointment, but it wasn't because of money," Leah said. "Canterbury was Ollie's second home. He was there daily, even after he finally had a degree in his pocket. I think he came alive under Jed Feller's tutelage. But anyway, Ollie had apparently told Chancellor Phillips that he'd will the house to Canterbury when he died. A place for the astronomy club to meet, he said."

"It's too bad. Canterbury would have maintained the house's integrity," Kate said.

"The university would have been a better choice than Tom Adler and his Prairie Development group," Po said. "They're saying Oliver also told them that they could have the house. They actually had a plan in place that they'd shown him. Tom promised he'd keep the lovely grounds as best he could, but the plan was to build four homes on the land—luxury homes for empty nesters."

"Ollie was so appreciative to people who were nice to him. I wonder if that's why he may have made promises like that," Leah said.

"Maybe," Po said. "But Max Elliot has handled some of the Harrington personal affairs, and he said Ollie never put anything like that in writing. I think Ollie cared more about things like black holes and planets' orbits than he did about wills. We used to laugh about that when I'd stop by and chat. He was pretty focused on the galaxy. He knew he stood apart from the college crowd but it didn't bother him."

"Have you been inside the Harrington home recently?" Leah asked.

"Maybe a few weeks ago? Well, not inside really. Most of the time the two of us would sit out on the back veranda and talk. The man could go on for hours about stars and gases and other-worldly bodies. I think he had read every book ever written on planet alignments. But he could talk about it in ways I completely understood. But as for the house, I haven't seen the inside of it since the senior Harringtons died."

"Would you like to?"

"To go inside?" Po asked. Although they usually took food to grieving families, the thought of taking a casserole to Adele Harrington brought a smile to both Po and Kate.

Leah laughed, too. "No, no pies or casseroles. Adele asked me to come by the house today to look at colors with her so I could order the fabric for the quilts she wants us to make. Want to come?"

"Of course," Kate said immediately. "Wow, a preview. I've wanted to see the inside of that house since I was a kid."

"I need to run by the college library briefly, but other than that I'm free until that reception tonight at the college," Po said. "Count me in."

"I nearly forgot about the reception," Leah said. "Eleanor is such a sport to host it. But at least that means it'll be less stuffy and more fun. I don't know what the college would do without her."

"Or the use of her house." The Canterbury family home had existed before Canterbury College itself, the school having grown up on the extensive acreage owned by the school's founders.

"I think the whole town must be invited," Kate said. "Even P.J."

"Even P.J.?" Po's voice was teasing. Kate's current relationship with the police detective was a roller coaster, and she was never sure where on the ride the two young people were. Po had known P.J. nearly as long as she'd known Kate: a kinder, more trustworthy man couldn't be found, but she tried very hard not to push it with Kate. Doing so would be a sure way of ruining it.

"Well, sure, P.J. would be invited," Leah said. "Eleanor figures her payback for hosting college affairs at her home is the license to invite all her friends. Besides, I think she has a crush on P.J."

They all laughed. "It may be vice versa," Kate said. "Have you seen those two at your house, Po? They're always cornering one another for some deep discussion about a political decision they both considered dumb or heinous, or a city council mess-up. Eleanor keeps P.J. current, too, making sure he knows about anything she thinks the police should be doing better. Not that he has anything to say about it."

"She told me she was inviting him to make sure the party was fun," Leah said.

Po laughed. "And he will. Those events can be mighty dull. I can't even remember what this one is for. Probably to showcase something going on at the college and hope it lures some of the invitees to donate to it."

"It's for a couple faculty members who have had things published recently. Jed Fellers, Ollie's mentor, is one of them," Leah said. "He's the main reason I'm going. Jed is such a nice guy. He's been working on getting a book published for the last couple years. There's so much pressure on faculty now that Canterbury has university status—even though we all still call it a college—that we're all overjoyed when someone makes it to print."

"Sounds kinda like *The Hunger Games*," Kate said.

"Sort of," Leah said.

"Well, good for Professor Fellers then. I took his intro to astronomy class just for the heck of it and it was great," Kate said. "He's a good teacher."

"Academia does have its pressure points. Scott used to bemoan it all the time. He'd be happy for Jed. And happy that Eleanor is still throwing celebratory parties."

"Yep. Uncle Scott would like this," Kate said, refusing to give up what she had always called Po's husband, even though no blood ties existed between the Paltrows and the Simpsons. What they had was stronger than blood ties, Kate's mother had always said.

"Well, no matter what the party's for, it'll get our minds off Adele Harrington for a while."

"Who seems to show up everywhere." Leah nodded toward a booth across the crowded aisle. Loaves of fresh homemade povitica from Kansas City's Strawberry Hill were piled on the table.

Po and Kate looked over.

Adele Harrington was talking to the young woman behind the table, all the while holding a loaf of the povitica in one hand. The girl's mother stood beside her, clearly listening to the conversation while helping another customer.

The younger woman was fidgeting, moving from one foot to another and casting sideways looks at her mother as if pleading for help. Finally, Adele shook her finger in the girl's face, set the loaf back down and abruptly turned and walked away. The young woman looked after her with tears in her eyes.

"Another fallen bird in Adele's path," Kate murmured. "Why does the woman treat people like that?" She wound her way across the crowded aisle and picked up the loaf of rich cream cheese bread. Adele's fingerprints were visible on the wrapping where she had squeezed it. She smiled at the young girl. "This looks terrific. How much?"

"Oh, wait, I'll get you a fresh one from the truck. This one has been squeezed, I'm afraid."

"Squeezing's fine. I'm okay with it. It'll taste just as good, right?"

The young girl smiled at Kate and fumbled in the large pocket of her apron for change. "So the lady—well, the one who squeezed it—she wants to give us some business, she said. She'll buy our poviticas for a bed and breakfast or something." She glanced at her mother. "So, well, I guess that's a good thing."

Her mother stepped over and wrapped an arm around her daughter's shoulder. She smiled at her, then looked at the women. "Something tells me we will earn every penny."

Kate laughed, and Po assured the baker that she definitely would do exactly that.

From several stalls up the aisle, Adele Harrington turned suddenly and looked over the heads of the crowd. Her eyes settled on Po and she called out to her over the market din.

Then, much to their relief, she followed it with a simple greeting, and turned in the opposite direction, walking away from the market, her head high.

Po watched her disappear, wondering with some sadness what was going on inside Adele Harrington's head. Kate's question was a good one. Why *did* she treat people with such disregard? But a stronger voice suggested she might be better off not knowing. She gathered up her cloth bags, heavy now with fall's bounty, and hurried after Kate and Leah.

Chapter 4

The Harrington mansion was noisy with activity when Po met Susan and Kate at the curb. The long winding drive that led up to the three-story stone house was lined with trucks, and men in overalls and jeans carried pails and heavy toolboxes. Fast-food wrappers and large drink cups cluttered the lawn.

"Geesh. Adele doesn't waste any time," Kate said, dodging a ladder swinging from a short, no-nonsense man's shoulder.

"The place is certainly getting a top-notch manicure," Po said.

"Just look at this place. Up close it's pure Gatsby," Kate mused. "All I need is a martini and a convertible."

Tall pines lined the perimeter and towering oak trees shaded the yard, their gnarled branches angling out in all directions. The tips of maple trees were beginning to turn red, a harbinger of fall. And everywhere, freshly tilled patches of earth boasted dozens of brilliant mums.

"You really don't get a proper sense of this place from the road," Leah said. "It's magnificent. I can't believe Ollie lived here all alone."

"I wonder if he was lonely," Po said, looking around. "He didn't seem to be, but I wonder…" She looked over at several men working in a shade garden along the side of the property near the garage, digging up the soil. Crates of flowers sat nearby. And just days ago she'd noticed volunteer trees, weeds, and overgrown bushes crowding the wrought iron fence. Today it was worked smooth, the rich soil holding hostas and red twig dogwoods and hydrangeas. It was like a movie set being constructed in a day. Unreal.

She glanced up at the apartment above the four-car garage, wondering if Joe Bates was still living there. The long-time gardener had been on staff at the Harrington home as long as she could remember, but she didn't see him in the group of young men working beneath the trees. Po liked Joe, a comfortable older man who had an amazing way with flowers. As unkempt as the property sometimes was in recent years, the small plots Joe got around to tending were always perfect. Sometimes, when she sat out back with Ollie, she'd see him puttering in his flowerbeds, one eye on the drive keeping watch for anyone who came near the house. Ollie's watchman. Today he was nowhere in sight.

"Looking for Miz Harrington?" a young painter called down to them as they approached the wide front porch. He was perched on a ladder, a paint can swinging precariously from a hook at the top.

"Yes," Leah answered. "Is she around?"

The man took off his baseball hat and wiped perspiration from his brow with the back of his hand. He pointed around the side of the house. "She's out back. Follow the roar and you'll find her easy enough. Not in the best of moods today, just a warning to y'all." He grinned, then tugged his cap back on and returned to painting the top edge of the porch.

The three women walked along the stone path that wound around the side of the house. Tall windows were flung wide open to catch the cool breezes of early fall, and the sounds of furniture being moved along with sanders grinding away on the hardwood floors poured out onto the grass.

Po shook her head, thinking of the amount of time she put into preparing for a simple lecture. How can Adele have planned and arranged all of this in such a terribly short time? Is it something that had been in the planning? But it couldn't have been. No one suspected Ollie's early demise. Perhaps if the money is right, she supposed, a phone might be all it would take to rush in work crews. That and an incredible organized person at the helm. Adele was proving to be exactly that.

"There's Adele," Leah said as they reached the back corner of the house. Spread out in front of them was a veritable park, thick stands of trees, a pond in the distance, paths and birdfeeders everywhere. Leah pointed to a gazebo nearly hidden in a grove of dogwood trees. Bright light cut through the branches and streamed paths of gold across the brick path.

Standing on one of the gold bricks was Adele, deep in conversation.

"Who's with her?" Po said, squinting in the sunlight as they walked toward the gazebo.

No one answered, but as they followed the winding path, their steps were slowed by Adele's voice, loud and clear—and definitely not happy. The painter had underreported what they were hearing around a thick band of mulberry bushes.

"Foolish, brazen young woman!" she hissed. "How dare you come to my home uninvited? And telling me about my brother? *My* brother. I'd like you to leave immediately. If I have to call the police, I will."

"But, please, Ms. Harrington. You need to understand," a softer voice replied. "I only want to help. Ollie was my friend. A *good* friend. He was terribly troubled about something. He should not have died." The woman's words were muffled in emotion.

"This is my house, and you are not making sense, young lady. Ollie didn't get upset about things. He was calm. Placid. Do not ruin his memory this way. You are out of line."

"Ollie was a decent, fine man. I know that as well as anyone. He was filled with goodness. And…" her voice was choked now. "And he was healthy. His heart was healthy. You know that and so do I. Ollie had no reason to die."

Just visible beyond the bushes and trees was a long narrow hand lifting in the air. Then just as abruptly, Adele let it fall to her side. She looked away from the woman, beyond her, to where the three women were trying unsuccessfully to be invisible. For a brief moment, she appeared disoriented, but in the next moment, a practiced smile spread across her long face. Not warm, but civil, cutting into the anger and pushing it aside.

"Good afternoon," Adele said evenly, stepping away from the woman. She glanced at a thin gold watch on her wrist. "You're on time, Leah. That's good. And Po and Kate, you are welcome as well." She walked down the three gazebo steps toward them, leaving an uncomfortable woman standing awkwardly behind her.

The younger woman was watching Adele walk away. Her face was tightened in anger, her hands clutching a battered backpack. For a brief moment, Po was afraid she was going to fling it at the back of Adele's head.

But instead, the ponytailed woman walked down the steps quickly, nodding politely at the three women and brushing past Adele Harrington. She stopped for just a second, a blush of embarrassment coloring her cheeks as she met Leah's smile of recognition. She started to speak, then pulled the words back and hurried along the path toward the house.

Po watched her walk away. Someone from the college? She looked vaguely familiar to her. But a brown ponytail and ordinary figure, jeans and a backpack bespoke of dozens of women she passed in Dillons Market or Marla's bakery or walking near the Emerald River every day.

The woman had slowed her step near the driveway. She paused, looking toward the garage as if expecting someone. Then Po noticed movement, too, and spotted a small familiar figure coming down the back stairs of the garage apartment.

Old Joe Bates. Po smiled, feeling relief that he was still around. Perhaps there was a softer side to Adele Harrington.

Joe was looking at the younger woman, smiling and waving her over.

But in the next instant, at the sound of Adele's voice, his head shot up and he stared at the small group walking toward the house.

Before Po could wave a hello, Joe turned and walked back to the garage, beginning what seemed to be an arduous trek up the stairs.

"We didn't mean to interrupt," Leah was saying to Adele.

"You didn't interrupt. We have an appointment, do we not?" Adele lifted one brow. She made no reference to the unpleasant encounter they had witnessed, and instead, waved them toward the house. "I want you to see the bedrooms. They're in a state of disrepair right now, but the colors are important. I think you will be able to feel the warmth and ambience and plan your quilts accordingly."

Po looked back once more. The young girl was gone. And Joe had finally reached the top of the garage stairs.

They walked through the French doors at the back of the house and around dozens of paint cloths and cans, ladders and boxes, and finally up a magnificent staircase to the second and third stories of the house. The place where guests would soon be catered to in the finest way.

"Amazing," Leah said, looking up at the elaborate carved moldings and high ceilings. "This is a beautiful home."

Adele nodded as she led them down a hallway. "There are twelve bedrooms, and each will have its own bath when finished. My father's study alone is large enough to be made into three of the rooms.

Po looked into one of the rooms, where a small sitting room would welcome guests before they entered into the bedroom beyond. It might have been a sewing room years before, or a nursery. Although some rooms were now stripped of furniture and rugs, and others were in a transition state, Po noticed some with personal items—books and pictures and writing materials cluttering tall secretaries and dressers and walnut armoires. A closet door, slightly ajar, showed dresses and silk robes hanging on hangers as if waiting for someone to wear them. She imagined it must look exactly like it did when Adele was a girl living at 210 Kingfish Drive. It looked like Ollie had left some things untouched, perhaps finding comfort in signs of his family.

As they wandered in and out of the rooms, Po wondered which one had been Oliver's. It was at the back of the house, she knew, because he often told her about standing at his window at night and seeing the stars reflected in the backyard pond.

"Oliver never wanted me to touch a thing after our parents died," Adele said, as if reading Po's thought. "As a result, the house is jam-packed with things. He never discarded anything. Every drawer is full. I am working away at it, little by little, but it will take years. It's like a massive garden allowed to grow unweeded and unwieldy."

She moved down the hallway and ushered the women into a room at the very end. This room was smaller than the others, and simply furnished with a single bed between two large windows, a dresser, several bookcases, and a desk. A large telescope was positioned in front of one of the windows, pointing toward the sky.

Po walked over and looked at the books on the shelves, mostly astronomy texts and readings about nature, all arranged alphabetically with their spines lined up perfectly on the shelf. "This is Oliver's room," she said quietly. "I can feel him here."

Adele stood right behind her, looking around. "This was the only room in the house that he would sleep in from the time he got his own bed. Oliver was as bright as they come, but a slight disorder made some things difficult for him. But you probably all knew that. Some people may have attributed his social interactions to being slow, but he was anything but. Ollie was brilliant." Her voice fell off, and she looked around the room, memories weighing visibly on her face. She picked up a book from the nightstand next to Ollie's bed. "Loren Eiseley, *Immense Journey*," she read.

"I always thought of Ollie as a kind of Loren Eiseley," Po said. "Part philosopher, part scientist. He had such a lovely way of describing the most complicated astronomical things." She looked at his desk, neat and orderly, a cup holding pencils on the side, a yellow pad of paper, and in the center of the desk, another book with a title that intrigued her: *A Plain Man's Guide to a Starry Night*. The cover looked new. She picked it up and leafed through it. New or not, Ollie must have liked it—the book was filled with underlined sentences and notes in the margins. She put it back in its place.

Adele looked around the room, taking in the neatly made bed, the bookcases, the straight-backed chair. She looked at Po with an unexpected softness in her eyes. "Whatever the design of the quilt you make for this room, it must have stars on it," she said softly. Then she straightened her shoulders and walked briskly out of the room. Kate and Leah followed her down the hall.

Po stood at the door for a minute, then looked at the narrow flight of steps just outside Ollie's door. A small landing with a window that looked over the backyard was visible before the stairs continued out of sight. *The steps that led to the kitchen?* she wondered. *The steps that led to Oliver's death?*

"Portia, are you coming?" Adele stood in the middle of the hallway, looking back at her.

Po turned back and smiled. "I was thinking about Oliver."

"And what were you thinking about him?"

"I was thinking that falling on those narrow stairs was a tragic way for him to die."

"But maybe fitting. An accident. Oliver's life, in a way, was an accident."

Po was startled by the unexpected anguish in Adele's voice. "Ollie was a good man. I doubt if he ever thought about his life as an accident," she said.

"I agree with Po," Leah said. "Ollie had a purpose to his life, especially these last few years. He spent time writing, and he had interesting conversations with students and faculty. He had a good life here, Adele."

Adele focused her attention on a Thomas Hart Benton painting leaning against the wall, not yet rehung after the wall was painted. Finally, she pulled her eyes away and looked at the three women now standing behind her. "Well, I hope so," she said, more to herself than the others. Then she abruptly began to walk down the hallway, ushering them back down the main staircase.

Adele moved through the back doors and out onto the veranda. "Breakfast will be served out here in nice weather," she said. "Would you like to have a cup of tea?"

Po glanced at her watch. "We've stayed longer than we intended."

"Eleanor's party," Kate yelped.

"I've kept you from something?" Adele asked, her brow lifting.

"No," Po assured her. "It's not until this evening. We'll be all right."

"All right for what?" Adele asked.

Po was uncomfortable. She felt fairly sure Eleanor hadn't invited Adele. She hadn't been here when the invitations went out. And her brother had just died. Inviting her to a party hardly would seem appropriate.

"Canterbury University is having a small reception tonight at Eleanor Canterbury's home," Leah explained. "It's done periodically to recognize faculty in one way or another."

"Who is being recognized?"

"Tonight it's faculty who have recently received awards or published something," Leah said. "Publishing is important to Canterbury, now that the college is a university."

"Publish or perish," Adele said.

"Kind of," Leah said. "Anyway, it's nice to recognize people who have done good work. And making a reception out of it can be a subtle push for others to follow."

Adele listened to Leah intently, a frown creasing her forehead. Then she shifted her attention, looking beyond the women, her thoughts seemingly moving on to other things. Finally she waved her hand in dismissal. "All right then. Please keep in touch with me about the quilts and your progress," she said. "And—"

A rattling noise near the driveway drew their attention to the garage. Joe Bates was pushing an old wheelbarrow filled with dirt across the walkway, the wheels wobbling and clumps of mud falling onto the brick pathway.

Adele's fingers curled into fists and her voice grew hard. "An eyesore," she muttered. And then, without another glance at her guests, she walked quickly down the patio steps and across the yard toward Joe.

For a moment, Po felt the need to beat her to her prey and to scoop old Joe Bates up and out of the way of Adele's anger. But before her resolution could take shape, Adele approached the man, her hands flying through the air and her muffled words burying him in a deluge of complaints.

"Let's get out of here," Kate said, heading down the side steps toward the driveway and their car. "We might be Adele's next target."

Po looked back. Adele was still ranting, but Joe Bates seemed to be oblivious to the onslaught. He was looking beyond her toward the pond, as if seeing something there that brought him pleasure.

Chapter 5

Po dropped Kate and Leah off and checked her watch. Enough time to get over to the library and pick up a new book on Kansas quilting circles that Leah had spotted and reserved for her. Women's work and projects during wartime was fascinating to her and had dominated her magazine and journal writing in recent years.

She pulled into the faculty lot and parked her car—a luxury that being married to a past university president afforded her—and climbed the wide fan of steps leading up to the massive library doors.

Jed Fellers pushed open the door from the other side and braced himself against it, holding it open for Po.

"Good to see you, Po. What brings you to our hallowed halls?" Jed shifted beneath the weight of an armful of books.

"Books, Jed, just like yourself. Speaking of books, I hear your first book is coming out. Congratulations. Is this research for number two?"

Jed laughed. "Maybe down the road. Definitely not now. I'm just trying to keep one step ahead of my students. That's a major task in itself. Canterbury has some smart kids."

"I hear Ollie Harrington was a friend of yours. And from what I know of him, he was one of those bright students."

Jed's smile faded. He nodded. "Ollie was many things to me—an assistant, a student, mostly a friend, I guess. He was…he was a breath of fresh air around here. He brought a charisma to a class. Such an honest guy, and certainly unique in his approach to the heavens." Jed looked out over the green lawns, now colored with small piles of falling leaves. "I'll miss the guy."

Sadness played across Jed's long features. Po wondered if Ollie had been aware of those he had touched. She suspected not. He was the twin less noticed, the second born, the one who had to work harder to make his place in life. But he had done a fine job of it. "From what I hear, you played an important role in his life," she said. "I would say you both benefited from the relationship."

Jed didn't answer, but he leaned over and lightly kissed her cheek. "Thanks, Po." He turned and slowly made his way down the library steps.

Po watched him through the thick glass of the door. His head was low, the books a weight in his arms. Now and then he'd look up and acknowledge a student's wave or greeting, and then continue on across the quad. Once he stopped and picked up a Frisbee that landed at his feet, tossing it back to a student and bowing slightly when she cheered his finesse.

Ollie was missed. But life went on. Po turned away from the door and walked into the main room of the library. It was busy today, and then Po remembered that midterms were probably around the corner. Some of the reason for Jed's burden of books, she supposed. She walked over to the reserve desk where Leah had left the book Po was looking for.

A pleasant-looking woman looked up and smiled as Po approached. She wore jeans and a T-shirt, her brown hair pulled back and held in place with a bright blue elastic band, her large framed glasses attractive. She looked familiar. And then Po remembered why.

Immediately the woman's smile faded. She looked down at the desk, embarrassed.

"Hi again," Po said. She looked at the nametag pinned to the woman's T-shirt. "Halley Peterson," she read. "I'm Po Paltrow."

The woman nodded. She looked even younger up close.

Halley adjusted her glasses and managed a small smile. "I apologize for that conversation you must have heard today. I saw you with Professor Sarandon. She's great, by the way. But I wasn't so great today." A slight blush colored her cheeks.

"You were fine and I'm sorry we eavesdropped. It was unintentional." Po wanted to ease her worry, to tell her she understood how difficult Adele could be. And to ask her more about her friendship with Ollie. She knew from Leah that Halley had returned to college belatedly and worked on campus to help pay her tuition. Leah had seen her with Ollie several times, but why she was at the Harrington home was a mystery.

Halley pushed her glasses into her hair. "Today hasn't been one of my best days. But Ollie Harrington was a good friend of mine. He spent a lot of time here in the library. Did you know him?"

"Yes. I don't live too far from the Harrington place. I used to visit Ollie. He was a good man."

"Yes, he was. And he would have loved a decent burial with his friends around him, telling Ollie stories. Missing him but grateful for knowing him. But Adele Harrington. His sister—" Halley broke off mid-sentence. She shook her head. "I'm sorry, I barely know you. You may be a friend of hers and I'm totally out of line speaking like this, Mrs. Paltrow."

"Please, Halley, call me Po. And I understand. Adele elicits strong responses in people. It's clear you cared about her brother. And maybe once the body is released she will reconsider a memorial."

Halley's face seemed to be crumbling under Po's concern. Slender fingers groped for a water bottle sitting on the counter beside a pad of paper.

"Maybe you should sit down, Halley," Po said. She touched her arm.

Halley shook her head. "I'm fine," she said softly. "But thank you." She leaned forward, her arms on the counter, her level gaze holding Po's attention. Her voice was low, but filled with a new sound, an intensity that for a moment startled Po and seemed out of place in the mild-mannered woman and in the quiet library.

"Someone needs to listen," Halley Peterson said. Her hands were shaking now, making small thumping noises on the library desk, her green eyes lit. "I don't think Ollie's death was normal. It wasn't right. I think…I think someone wanted Ollie Harrington to die."

Chapter 6

Po had had no time to respond. Several students needing Halley's attention had cut short her conversation with the librarian. She checked out her book and left the library.

But Halley's words stayed with her, ringing in her ears. Surely she didn't mean the words literally. She was emotional. A friend had died and she hadn't had a chance to say goodbye. But the short conversation left Po disturbed and her head cluttered with questions.

She checked her watch, wishing she had time to go back into the library when Halley was free. But it was late. And she had just enough time to get ready for Eleanor's cocktail party before Max Elliot, the always prompt attorney and financial advisor, picked her up.

A quick shower helped wash away the niggling feeling she carried home. A pair of silky black slacks and a bright blue wraparound blouse made her feel at least a semblance of festivity. She ran a brush through her hair, ignored the strands of gray woven through it, and glanced briefly in the full-length mirror, ensuring nothing was out of place.

"Po, you up there?" Max Elliot stood at the foot of the staircase, one hand on the walnut post. "It's time to go. And what did I tell you about locking these doors? I could have run off with everything."

A bark accompanied his words and Po laughed. Hoover wasn't much of a watchdog, but he loved her. And also most of the people who came through the unlocked doors.

"I'll be down in a minute," Po called back, ignoring the gentle scolding, even though his comment didn't come out of the blue. It had only been a year since she and Max had both been in danger when someone entered her home through the open front door. And although she wouldn't give Max the satisfaction by telling him, she did lock her doors. Sometimes.

Po swept blush across her cheekbones and she was nearly set to go. Grabbing a black shawl from the back of a chair, she headed down to a waiting Max.

"If I had locked the door, dear Max," she said with a grin, "how could you possibly have gotten in?"

Max sighed and kissed her on the cheek, the familiar answer lost in the pleasure of seeing her. "I would have broken it down to see you. You look lovely, by the way."

A friend of both Po and her husband Scott's for as long as Po could remember, Max had become a trusted confidant when Scott died, helping Po sort through the investments and trusts Scott had left.

But in recent months the two had slipped into a habit of attending movies and lectures and social gatherings together, and Po admitted to Leah recently that the nice-looking widower with the quick wit was adding a new, surprising dimension to her life. "The heart can still somersault a bit," she had confessed, although she wasn't sure she wanted it to be much more than that. Scott Paltrow still lived in her heart and her home and her life—and she wasn't sure there was room in those places for anyone else.

* * * *

The ride to Eleanor's was short and Po and Max drove in comfortable silence, speaking only when the lights from the large three-story house on the corner of the Canterbury campus lit up the night. In the distance, the ivy-covered campus buildings rose like silhouettes against the darkening sky.

Max pulled into the long circle drive, parking behind a black SUV. "It looks like a full house."

"That's our Eleanor—she loves her family home coming alive." Although tonight's event was officially a college function, Eleanor never hesitated to add her own guest list to the official one when she was opening the doors of Canterbury House for the event. It was her prerogative, she claimed, and no one complained. And with one of the honorees this evening being a popular professor, the crowd was bound to be colorful, eclectic, and noisy.

They walked into the mix of voices and laughter, accompanied by a small jazz combo playing a medley of old Ray Charles tunes. If Eleanor had her way, which she surely would, Po knew the music would become livelier once the evening progressed.

Kate and P.J. were standing in the high-ceilinged living room, just off the front hall, talking with Jed Fellers. Kate's two-inch heels brought her green eyes up to P.J.'s level.

Po swallowed the pleasure that being Kate's godmother brought her on a continuous basis, even when she and Kate were at odds, which happened when Po tried to decide what was best for Kate. And most often Kate treated her the same way she had her own mother: with great love sometimes peppered with irritation.

Po hugged her tightly, hiding the sudden spurt of emotion that sometimes overwhelmed her when she thought of Kate's mother. She missed her best friend as much today as when she had died nearly four years earlier.

Kate finally wiggled free. "Yes, I miss her too," she whispered to her godmother.

Po turned toward the tall, lanky professor standing across from her. "What a treat, seeing you twice in one day. Congratulations again."

"Thanks for coming, Po. You, too, Max. It was nice of the college and Eleanor to do this—it's great to see old friends."

"Eleanor loves an excuse for a party. And you are part of a very nice excuse."

Max shook Jed's hand. "Sounds like the pressure is on at the university to publish. Good for you. And for the record, it's a great book. I got an advanced reader's copy."

Jed nodded. "The publisher sent out a slew of those. Niggling for reviews and booksellers' attention."

Kate picked up a copy of Jed's book from a table displaying it. "*A Plain Man's Guide to a Starry Night,*" she said out loud. "Well, that's me, for sure. I will be a perfect test case."

Jed laughed. "Katie, you are anything but plain."

P.J. wrapped on arm around her shoulders, agreeing. "According to our favorite bookstore owner, the book isn't plain either. Gus Schuette is devoting the whole window to you. It looks interesting. Astronomy has always been a secret passion of mine."

"Oh?" Kate turned her head and looked up into P.J.'s face. Her brows lifted. "A passion?"

"Well, secondary passion," P.J. said. He tugged lightly on a loose strand of Kate's hair.

Hearing his name, Gus Schuette walked over to the group. "It's a terrific book," he boomed. "And I know books. Even the *Times* agrees with me."

Jed's face colored slightly. "It's just a little book. The fuss is unmerited."

"Well, big or little, it will be nice to have the university's publishing pressure off your back for a while," Max said.

"Here, here," said Jed, lifting his glass. "That I will definitely toast to."

"Ah, my friends are here." Eleanor walked up behind the professor. "The party can now begin. Good. Sometimes the university crew is a little boring." She kissed Jed on the cheek. "You excluded, my dear."

"I think that's a compliment," Jed said. "El, you're nice to do this."

"Pshaw with nice. I love it. It's a chance to be merry. We needed a diversion, Jed, and you and the others have stepped into the excuse role nicely."

"You mean Ollie's death," Jed asked. "I agree with that. Even my students are feeling it."

"Yes, of course. But in addition, I think the whole town is in an uproar over Adele Harrington and the house everyone and his brother seem to want." Eleanor waved to an old friend walking in the door, excusing herself and playing the hostess.

"The commotion over the Harrington house is curious," Max said. "Folks have disagreed with property sales and zoning laws before, but this is out of proportion."

"Well, there's a lot of money at stake," Gus said.

"Sure—but the land belongs to Adele, clean and clear. Tom Adler over at Prairie Development had me check—he claims Oliver promised to sell the house to him for a development. Says he saw the paper himself."

"Tom Adler?" Kate said. She took a piece of crisp pita topped with a sliver of rare tuna from a passing waiter.

"Adler claims Oliver wrote it out, like a will," Max said. "Ollie didn't want Adele to get the house, according to Tom, and they were going to sign an agreement that would allow Oliver to live in the house free and clear as long as he liked, then Tom would take it over. But there's nothing I can find that even hints at that." Max took a drink of his bourbon and then added, "Tom claims someone should check more closely into how Oliver died. I told him suggestions like that could do damage in a town this size and his disappointment could be handled some other way."

Po listened to the conversation around her with interest, her thoughts returning to Halley Peterson and the sentiment Po had dismissed as the voice of grief. *Oliver didn't die from a fall down the stairs,* she had implied.

P.J. returned to the group carrying a tray of champagne and stood between Kate and Po. "What are you worried about, Po?"

"Conversations like this are worrisome. Perhaps if Ollie's body could be released and a memorial service held, people might settle down and we might all feel some closure."

P.J. nodded, but his silence was an uncomfortable one.

Kate looked at him, frowning. "It's not like you not to offer an opinion. What gives? Has Adele taken care of everything and we simply don't know about it?"

"Everything?" P.J. asked, avoiding the question.

"You know what I'm asking. Has the body been released?"

"Soon," he said.

"Well now, that's just plain odd," Eleanor said. She'd come up behind them quietly, listening to the conversation. "Let the poor man rest in peace. It was a heart attack, plain and simple."

P.J. felt his pocket as a vibrating cell phone interrupted their talk. He pulled it out and glanced at the number on the small screen, then looked up. "Sorry folks, gotta take this." He moved to a quiet corner to take the call.

Another waiter passed by, carrying a platter of chicken satay with a crystal cup of gingery peanut sauce. Small plates were passed around, and the group quickly emptied the tray.

"Eleanor, you certainly know how to throw a party," Kate said, balancing her plate in one hand and finding a tall table to set down her glass of champagne. "This is terrific."

"The house should be used this way. One old soul doesn't do justice to it," Eleanor said. "It was what old Grandpop Canterbury intended. He loved nothing better than a good party."

Po laughed and looked up at the enormous portrait of Harrison Canterbury hanging over the fireplace. White hair perfectly coiffed. Strong cheekbones and a serious chin. But the artist had caught an adventurous glint in his eyes that perfectly mirrored the one in his daughter Eleanor's.

Harrison had built his elegant home over a century before, after he had moved his family from the east to the small Kansas town. A much better place to raise kids, he had told anyone who asked. And having inherited a fortune as a railroad baron's son, he soon built Crestwood a bank, a department store, and a church, and prettied up the city with several parks. But once his children were older, Harrison decided that what the town really needed was a college, and so he built one, right in the family's wooded backyard. Though the home belonged to the Canterburys until they all died, Eleanor insisted the home remain an active part of the college, just as Harrison Canterbury himself had done.

"Well, I'll be," Kate said, pausing between bites to stare at the front door. "Look who's here."

Po glanced over. The double doors were left open as guests came and went and her view was blocked by a couple headed toward the exit. When they moved on, Po stared into the hallway. "Well, that's a surprise," she said.

Adele Harrington stood alone, tall and elegant in a periwinkle silk dress. Her hair was down, falling loosely about her shoulders and held back from her face by a small ebony comb. It was a transformation that drew unintentional sounds from Kate and Po. "What happened to the wicked witch of the north?" Kate whispered.

Though not beautiful in a traditional sense, Adele was striking tonight, her imposing manner heightened by careful makeup and clothing. She stood alone, like an actor on a stage looking out over her audience.

"With her recent loss, I didn't think she would want to come," Eleanor said softly. "But everyone is welcome to these things. I'm happy she came."

Although she couldn't have heard Eleanor's kind words, Adele turned at that moment and spotted the small group, acknowledging them with a careful smile. She walked their way. "Hello, everyone. Po, Kate, Max." She nodded to Gus, and then focused on her host. "This is a lovely party, Eleanor."

"It's a happy group. And I for one, am so pleased you came, Adele." Eleanor looked at Jed. "Do you and Professor Jed Fellers know one another? He's one of our excuses for having this affair."

Jed shook Adele's hand and bowed slightly.

"Yes, we've met," Adele said.

"When Ollie won the award for his essay," Jed said. "I remember. What I remember especially is how happy he was that you came."

Adele looked pleased.

"I haven't had the opportunity to tell you how sorry I am, Adele," Jed went on. "I'll miss your brother. He was a student of mine, but really more than that. Ollie was an inspiration to my students." Jed paused, then said, "Ollie was my friend."

"Yes, I know that," Adele said. Her voice softened, but only slightly. And then she turned back toward Eleanor and acknowledged that she hadn't been invited. "But I was sure you wouldn't mind. I wanted to be around people who knew Ollie."

"Of course," Eleanor said. "You are welcome here. Always. And there are many people here who will be pleased to meet you. Come." She took Adele's arm and turned her away, introducing her to a passing couple that taught at the college.

"Where's P.J?" Kate whispered to Po.

Po stepped away, looking around the groups of people. "I saw him reach for his phone as Adele walked in. Then he disappeared."

Taller than Po by an inch or two, Kate peered over the tops of heads. "Found him," she said, pointing toward the foyer.

P.J. spotted them at the same time and wove his way over, circling groups as if he were in a hurry. His face was tight, brows pulled together.

"P.J., what's wrong?" Kate's smile faded when she looked into the concern clouding his face.

"I have to leave," he said softly. "Bad news." He looked around, then motioned Kate and Po over to a quiet spot at the edge of the fireplace. "It's what we were expecting. But it's finally confirmed and will soon be public knowledge. Ollie didn't have a heart attack. He was poisoned."

A sound behind them seemed to accompany P.J.'s muted awful words.

Three steps away, standing alone and looking up at the portrait of the founder of Canterbury College, Adele Harrington stiffened at the sound of her brother's name. And then, as if it had taken those few seconds for P.J.'s words to settle in a proper order that gave them meaning, her strong shoulders sagged and a sigh escaped her lips, the sound of trapped air escaping.

"Adele—" Po took a step toward her, her hand outstretched.

But before she could touch her, Adele Harrington's carefully held-together body caved in on itself and began to slide, folding up like a rag doll in the center of Eleanor's thick crimson Gabbeh rug.

Chapter 7

The gossip surrounding Adele Harrington's new bed and breakfast paled in the wake of the news that her brother had been murdered.

"I never thought I would feel sorry for Adele Harrington," Selma Parker said, smoothing out a stretch of fabric on her cutting table. "But my heart goes out to the poor woman. I can't imagine what she's going through."

"My thoughts exactly. It doesn't make sense. Ollie was a kind, simple man who would never hurt anyone." Po stood at the counter in the quilt shop, watching Selma cut into the deep blue fabric. "I can only imagine how heavy her heart is." Po rummaged in her purse for her wallet.

Thoughts of Ollie had stayed with her through the night, pushing sleep aside. She'd finally driven away the sad thought and used the time to imagine his quilt—*her* quilt, the one she would put together for him. The one that would bring sweet thoughts of him alive and block out the awfulness of his death.

She had imagined the perfect pattern, a multitude of stars of every shape. And with Selma's help they'd found fabric in golds, rusts, and deep, rich greens to make the quilt come to life in the small clean room that had been Ollie's.

"These colors are perfect. It's almost as if Ollie helped us pick them." Selma folded the pieces into a neat pile and slipped them into a bag. "It must have been an awful scene last night at the Canterbury house."

Po handed Selma her credit card. She nodded. "Max and I took Adele home. By the time we got her inside and poured her a shot of brandy, she was thinking clearly and suggested strongly that we leave. I think she's denying this horrible news. She tried to make light of her fall, saying something about crashing Eleanor's party—then having it crash her. But as hard as she tried to hide her emotion, there was pure agony in her eyes."

"She's a gutsy gal," Selma said. "She'll get through this no matter how tough it is."

"Well, she appears strong on the surface anyway."

Susan walked in from the back room and piled a stack of bags beneath the checkout counter. "Have the police learned anything more? I stopped at Marla's bakery this morning and the buzz was as thick as her syrup. It isn't that everyone knew Ollie—but everyone knows that house. The Harrington name. And Adele has been irritating people enough that those who didn't know it, do now. The rumors are rampant."

"Marla thrives on all that. I'm sure she has the crime solved and wrapped up in a blue ribbon. I don't think the official news is quite so clear-cut."

"Has P.J. said anything?" Susan asked.

"I talked to Kate earlier this afternoon. P.J. said it's kind of a mess. All the work being done on the house will make it nearly impossible to get any kind of prints. But they've already started to canvass the neighborhood, questioning people, along with others who had access to Ollie's house. He didn't have a lot of people coming in and out but there were a few repairmen in the last couple weeks. A mailman. And old Joe Bates was out there in the garden every day."

"And he lived right there, above the garage. He was devoted to Ollie. Maybe he'll shed some light on all this, although his hearing isn't what it used to be," Selma said.

"I can't imagine anyone wanting to hurt that sweet man," Susan said. "I used to talk to him sometimes at the college. If he wasn't sitting in on a class, he was almost always in the library or in the commons, writing on his yellow pads."

"What did he write about?" Po asked.

"I don't know—things he learned in class, I guess. He hung on every word that came out of Professor Fellers's mouth. Ollie loved learning. And if you ask me, he loved that librarian, too."

Po's head went up. "Librarian? Who?"

"Halley something. A nice gal. She's worked in the library for a couple of years. She takes classes, too. I think she and Ollie were friends. I saw them a few times together, out in the quad eating sandwiches and talking."

"I met her the other day," Po said. "Twice, actually." She repeated the brief conversation she'd had with Halley in the library. "When I saw her earlier at the Harringtons', it seemed she was working through the emotions you have when a friend dies—reaching out for answers and trying to make sense of it all. I thought coming to see Adele was maybe her way of dealing with things. And her comment about Ollie not having a heart attack sounded like a denial to herself. He couldn't be dead because he had a strong heart, the kind of thing we say when we don't want to accept reality. Adele didn't want to hear any of it. But now it seems Hallie meant exactly what she was saying."

Susan leafed through some receipts, then looked up. "Adele's name has already been thrown into the mess of people who suddenly looked suspicious. At least according to Marla."

The bell at Selma's front door jingled as several customers walked in. Selma looked over, then handed back Po's credit card. "We need to talk about this more," she said. "Like I said, Adele Harrington isn't my favorite person, but I can't imagine she had anything to do with Ollie's death. She didn't show her face around here until his body was already in the morgue. So unless she snuck in town without anyone seeing her, she couldn't have done it. And besides that, he was her twin brother. Good grief. She's no Medea." Selma shook her head, then tucked a loose gray strand behind her ear and walked off to help a young woman find some Irish lace.

"What do you think, Po?" Susan asked.

"I think this town doesn't need a lingering crime on its hands. I hope the police solve it immediately, if not sooner. And frankly, I agree completely with Selma. I know police often look at family first, but I can't imagine that Adele Harrington had a thing to do with her brother's death."

"The rumors aren't going to help her bed and breakfast business any."

"No, I suppose not. It's a shame, too. So let's hope the crime is solved soon and we can all return to business as usual."

Po slipped the package of fabric into her tote and left the shop. She walked down Elderberry Road toward the bakery for a bag of sourdough rolls for dinner. But the thought of stepping into a pit of rumors slowed her step and made her consider cutting back on bread.

She paused at a rapping sound coming from the front window of Jacques's French Quarter restaurant. She glanced over into the welcoming face of Max. He was holding up a martini glass and motioning for her to come in.

Po glanced at her watch. Almost five. The thought of a drink with a friend greatly surpassed sourdough rolls and rumors, and Po smiled back, then pushed open the heavy restaurant doors.

The bar in Jacques's bistro was separated from the larger dining area by a few leafy ferns. As Po walked around them to the cocktail area, she saw that it wouldn't be a quiet drink with Max after all. He was holding out a chair at a table for four near. P.J. and Jedson Fellers, deep in conversation, were already seated.

They looked up as Po's shadow fell across the table.

P.J. half stood and kissed her cheek. "Glad you're here, Po."

Po touched his shoulder lightly. "Tough day, I know." She dropped her purse on the floor and sat down. A young waiter appeared as if by magic and set a perfectly chilled martini down in front of her. She glanced around at their faces. "You're talking about Ollie's death." *Death*. She still couldn't call it a *murder*, as if not saying the word might change the realty. But maybe something had happened, some missing piece discovered that would change the awful news of the night before. "What's happened?"

"The investigation is in full force," P.J. said, seeing the hope of good news on Po's face and not wanting to mislead her. "But there's no news, not really. Not yet."

"But there is good news from the college so we're taking what we can get," Jed said. "A chunk of change was given to Canterbury University in memory of Ollie, and the board decided to establish a scholarship fund in his name. I was asked to pull something together. Max and P.J.—newest member of the university board—are helping."

Po smiled at the news, pleased that someone had been able to think beyond the awfulness of how Ollie died to something that would honor the person. "This will mean a lot to Adele, especially with the ugliness surrounding her life right now."

"Ollie deserves the honor," Jed said. "But I think Adele Harrington just wants all this put to rest. That's understandable, too."

Po nodded. If she was guessing correctly, this was almost as hard on Jed Fellers as it was on Adele. Even though Ollie was only a handful of years younger than Jed, he had been the younger man's mentor, a kind of father figure, maybe, and the sadness in the professor's eyes was evident.

"Adele isn't accepting the fact that Ollie was murdered," P.J. said. "She isn't cooperating in the investigation. She doesn't want to talk to anyone in a uniform."

Max agreed. "But I called her earlier and told her about the scholarship. I think she appreciated it." He went on telling them all about some of the ways they could legally put it together.

Po sipped her martini and listened to them talk about the details. She had little to add and her thoughts kept turning to Adele. To losing a brother. To dealing with the complicated waves of grief. She could understand Adele's feelings in wanting to erase the realty of murder. It was ugly. Unnatural.

Ollie was dead. There wasn't anything anyone could do about that. So let him rest in peace, as the church fathers prayed.

But the facts were what they were. That someone in their quiet peaceful town might have been responsible for ending Oliver's life far too early.

A crowd was gathering in the restaurant as folks stopped in after work for a drink and Jacques's truffles. The buttery aroma of escargot filled the air, and Po looked over the ferns to see Jacques placing a platter in front of Crestwood's successful developer. Tom Adler sat across from his new wife, Cindy. The restaurant owner loved the drama of his food, and he set the escargot down with a flourish, his flushed face beaming with delight over his prized appetizer.

He caught Po looking over and winked, then soon edged his way over to her table. "My magnificent Po—" He kissed her lightly on each cheek, then straightened up, looking around the table and greeting the others, his expression turning grave. "Such talk going on. All over my restaurant tonight. It's like a poison. People pointing fingers. People angry. Some angry even at poor dead Ollie. 'What bad thing did he do?' they ask. He must have done something bad for someone to kill him." He shook his head in disgust, small strands of silvery hair moving across a mostly bald head.

Po looked over at Tom Adler, now relishing the rich delicacies making their way to his mouth. A river of butter ran down his chin.

Jacques followed her look. "Tom is my good customer. And he is so upset. He wasn't the one who killed Ollie, he told me so. But he might know who did."

P.J., Jed, and Max looked up.

"He said some awful things about Ollie's sister," Jacques went on. "She is his twin, *non*? He says she's destroying Ollie's *maison* and he is surely rolling around in his grave."

"Sure, Tom's upset about all this," P.J. said. "He's come into the station a couple of times, trying to get the police to stop the renovations. He says the land is his, like you said, Jacques. But—"

"*Oui*," Jacques said, his arms flying in the air. "There's a piece of paper somewhere in the house that confirms it. But Mademoiselle Adele won't let him past the front door."

Max glanced over at Tom, then back to Jacques. "I'd suggest you don't take everything you hear as gospel truth. Tom is a good developer but he has a tendency to rant. And he'd better watch those rantings. They present a motive for murder, whether he sees it that way or not." He took a drink and shook his head. "His company is having a rough year. Developing the Harrington property—and he'd probably do a good job of it—would put him back on his feet. But I can't imagine why Ollie would have promised it to him."

Jacques leaned over and dropped his voice to avoid being heard beyond their table. "He pestered Oliver all the time, that much I saw myself. He brought him in here a few times and tried to get him drinking, but Ollie didn't ever touch a drop. Not once. Oliver's only libations were milk and tea. Tea and my escargots," Jacques said, his eyes rolling and one hand slapping a round cheek that wobbled beneath the touch. "Ma mere would turn over in her grave."

Po had seen Ollie in Jacques's once or twice herself—and a few other places on Elderberry Road. And sometimes with Tom, just as Jacques was saying. But the idea of trying to inch one's way into someone's inheritance—especially when that someone wasn't elderly and seemed to be in good health—was hard for her to get her arms around.

And to murder for it?

But murder was illusive and didn't always follow the rules of logic. Po knew how difficult it could be to walk in someone else's shoes. To understand the power of rage or fear or even love that might push someone to the edge.

She looked over at Tom Adler again. He had stopped eating when a city council member approached his table. They were talking heatedly, with Tom's head shaking and one hand waving in the air. Po could tell he'd had a few drinks and it wasn't helping his composure any. But she'd known Tom long enough to know his bark was stronger than his bite. Or so she'd always thought. Next to him, his wife looked bored and seemed to be entertaining herself by admiring the large diamond decorating her finger.

Catching Po's look, Tom nodded at her, forcing a slight smile to his face. A few minutes later, he slapped down a few bills, and he and his bride left the bistro abruptly, brushing aside a young waiter as they hurried through the door.

Po watched him through the window as they crossed Elderberry Road, Tom several steps ahead of Cindy. He barely noticed a car that nearly sideswiped his wife, then climbed into a big truck parked in front of Max's law office. Seconds later gravel shot out from under the tires as he tore off down the street.

An angry man.

"Mon Dieu!" Jacques said beside her, startling Po from her thoughts. But he wasn't watching Tom's hasty exit; he was staring at the front door.

Po followed his look. Adele Harrington stood just inside the door, her hair uncharacteristically mussed, her hands on her hips. Her face was a mixture of anger and determination, and her eyes immediately settled on Po.

Adele lifted one hand in a semblance of a wave.

Seeing Adele's flushed face and having so recently picked the woman's crumbled form from a floor, Po didn't hesitate to push away from the table just in case Adele needed help. Fainting in Jacques's crowded bistro would be too heavy a burden for Adele to bear.

But before she could reach her side, Adele took another step into the room and focused on P.J.

"Officer Flanigan," she called across the crowded bar, "I need to talk to you. Immediately, if you don't mind."

Chapter 8

Po reached her first. "Adele, are you all right?"

"No, Portia, I am not all right. Would you and P.J. please come with me."

It wasn't a question and the two began to follow her outside. P.J. sent an apologetic shrug to a confused Max and Jed.

Adele walked a few steps away from the door and stopped, taking in a deep, breath. "Someone," she said at last, "has been in my house."

Po waited, expecting more.

But Adele was silent, her looking moving from one to the other.

P.J said, "Adele, there are dozens of people in your house every day."

Adele cast him an impatient look. "Someone," she said, dismissing the comment with a clipped tone, "broke into my house during the night. Paint was spilled, furniture was damaged. Pictures thrown on the floor."

"Are you sure it wasn't a workman's error?" Po asked. "Paint could easily have been spilled."

"Please, spare me," Adele said. She turned to P.J. "I said that someone is breaking the law. You are the law, are you not?"

"Have you called the station?" P.J. asked. "There are police assigned to watching your house and to…to this case, Adele, and they—"

Adele held out her hands to quiet him. "I wanted to talk with someone I know personally. Police are annoying. I called Kate Simpson, and she told me I would find you here. Now, what are we going to do about this?"

"Was anything taken?"

"Not that I could tell. But how would I know? The house is a mess. Things everywhere."

"I'll see that someone comes out to investigate the damage, Adele, and you'll have to file a report."

"No. I don't want reports. What I want is for this to stop, Flanigan. I have felt for several days that things were not right in the house. Things were askew. Moved around. In some of the rooms I have kept family things intact to create ambiance. Things have been disturbed, I could feel it."

"Were you in the house last night?" Po asked. "Did you hear anything?"

"I wasn't there. The paint smell was horrible so I was staying at that Canterbury Inn on campus. But I won't do that again. I would certainly have heard the vandals and put a stop to it myself."

P.J. listened, his thoughts moving back to the night before. It had been one of those near-perfect, Indian summer nights, and he and Kate had taken a late-night walk beneath a deep canopy of stars. They'd stopped for sushi at a new little restaurant near the river, filled with college students taking a break from cramming for mid-terms—and then they had walked back through the Elderberry neighborhood and down Kingfish Drive, right past the Harrington home. It had been quiet. They'd even stopped in front of it for a few minutes, admiring the recently planted gardens along the drive. They were lit by a row of low lights that might have been installed just that day. And they'd remarked on all Adele had done in just a few days. Kate had thought the frantic activity was Adele's panacea for grief.

The big stone house loomed large in the background, lit softly with security lights and the stars from above. The only inside lights they could see came from the back garage apartment that Joe Bates lived in. And while they stood at the end of the drive, those lights went out, too, and they saw Joe come out of the apartment and light up a cigar beside the garage. At risk of disturbing his privacy, they had walked on down the street.

"We walked by your house last night, Adele," P.J. said aloud. "It was quiet."

"I don't care about quiet," Adele snapped. "Sometime last night, somehow, someone did damage inside my house, and it has to stop. You are the police, do something."

"Joe Bates was there. He may have heard something. Have you talked with him?"

"Joe Bates's hearing is less than a slug's. As soon as I have time to think about replacing him, I will do so. He's only around because my mother and my brother took pity on him."

"He's a wonderful gardener, Adele," Po said quickly. It was true. He'd nurtured her own garden one summer; everything he touched in it turned to beauty. Adele's disdain for such a gentle old man was hurtful.

Adele's expression crumbled slightly, the stern look giving way. "How can he be here, alive, moving around. When my brother is dead?"

Of course. Adele was giving voice to grief, not hatred. Perhaps days would soften her resolve.

Before she could move beyond her thoughts, Adele spun around on heels Po wouldn't dream of wearing, and she was gone.

They watched in surprised silence as she walked across Elderberry Street, ignoring a driver that honked as he swerved to miss her

When she reached her car, she paused and looked back at Po and P.J. as if knowing they'd still be standing there, watching her.

"I'm not a fool, Po Paltrow," she called across the street. "I am very aware that there are people in this town who, number one, want me out of here, and secondly, want my property. But neither of those things are going to happen. And I will prosecute anyone who stands in my way." She opened the door and slid in behind the wheel. In the next minute, she was gone, driving far too fast for the quiet neighborhood shopping area.

Po shook her head. "There's something very sad about that woman."

"Nasty, is more like it," P.J. said. He shoved his hands in his jeans' pockets and looked up at the sky. "I think I need something really nice to get rid of the taste."

"Like Kate?" Po asked.

P.J. laughed. "Now you're a mind reader, Po. Scary."

"Will you follow up on Adele's claims?"

He nodded. "I'll make a call to the station and have someone go out to the house. And then I think I'll see if Katie has any of her grilled salmon and orzo salad lying around looking for someone to eat it."

Po laughed and looked into P.J.'s clear blue eyes. They were quite bright these days. That not only made her happy, it would delight Kate's mother, though she might have preferred he stuck to practicing law than turning to police work. Liz Simpson's daughter's safety was always her topmost issue, mostly because her daughter wasn't a very good judge of danger."

"Think you can handle the men in there by yourself?" P.J. nodded toward the bistro window where Max now stood, hands in his pockets and peering out, a puzzled look on his face.

Po turned and waved. "I'll fill them in on Adele's concern, and then I am heading home myself."

Home. It was the only place she wanted to be right now. Alone on her screened porch with Hoover at her side. Alone to watch the sky darken, to talk to Scott up there somewhere.

And to sort through the days that had suddenly robbed her of the peace that the small town of Crestwood had always wrapped her in.

Chapter 9

"What do you think, ladies?" Phoebe held up a finished block for her quilt.

"Phoebe, that's wonderful!" Kate set her coffee cup down and leaned across the table to see the colorful green and pink flowered block. Phoebe was using the butterfly pattern from one of the *Kansas City Star's* quilt books. She'd chosen playful calico prints in pink, bright reds, greens, and yellows.

Kate looked more closely. "Except for that bit of goldfish cracker stuck to a butterfly wing."

She flicked it away and Phoebe hooted.

"It's the world I live in," she said. "But except for the goldfish, I think it's pretty cool myself."

"Adele wanted at least one crib quilt. That was thoughtful of her, don't you think?" Selma said. "Phoebs, you're the perfect person to make it."

"Perfect, hah. Jimmy is getting worried. We're about to move Jude and Emma into youth beds, and Jimmy knows it's painful for me to have an empty crib in the house. When he saw me working on this block he, like, freaked. He turned as white as Eleanor's hair."

Eleanor laughed and patted Phoebe's hand. "You are a good mom, Phoebe dear. You should have twenty little ones."

"Twenty little what?" Susan asked, coming into the sewing room.

"Phoebe's deciding her future," Po said. "And while she does, let's see your quilt, Susan. It's for that gigantic king-sized bed in the tower suite, right?"

Susan opened a cabinet and pulled out a stack of finished blocks. The pile of colors—yellow gold, greens, silvery blues and grays, and deep pinks—was remarkable, even without being set in a design. "Adele wanted something different in that room—something contemporary—so I didn't use a traditional pattern."

"Susan, you could scatter those colors on a bed just like they are and you'd create a beautiful tapestry," Po said.

Susan smoothed out one of the blocks. "Adele—believe it or not—had a trunk filled with gorgeous silk fabrics. She'd collected them from her travels all over the world. We went through it together and I pulled these out for the quilt."

Selma stood next to Susan and looked closely at the design sketched on the piece of paper. "I think people will pay to stay in this room for the quilt alone. It's gorgeous, honey."

Strips of gray and blue would form the border, and in the center a vibrant swirl of pink, spiraling out into yellows and golds drew everyone's attention. The design was all movement and color. "I went over to check the paint color and figure out the border. The house is really coming along," Susan said. "Kate went along to keep me company."

"To nose around is more like it," Kate said. "The Harrington house fascinates me and when Adele showed us through, I wasn't able to snoop. It always intrigued me, even when I was little, although it frightened me back then. The Harringtons were so private. And after the parents died, Ollie sometimes let the house go, with weeds all over."

Phoebe nodded. "Some of my playgroup moms refused to take their kids trick or treating over there. Silly. Ollie was harmless. But the house did look a little like Boo Radley's house in *To Kill a Mockingbird*—frightening and mysterious—"

"But holding something decent," Kate added. "And now the house is beautiful—"

"But that something decent is missing," Po said. "At least in the person of Ollie."

Kate nodded. "It's sad. And unnerving, and until the guy who did this is caught, the real beauty of that house can't come through. It just can't. It's messing up the town. We need to end it."

"Kate," Po said. The single word held a warning, and everyone in the room could hear it in Po's soft tone.

"There's no danger, Po," Susan said with a smile. "None of us are going to become vigilantes. Not even Kate."

"All right, I overreact sometimes. But someone has been murdered, Susan. We can't take that lightly."

"But surely it's someone far removed from us. And sure, he or she needs to be caught, but I don't think any of us are in danger. Whoever did it is probably a world away by now. The life Ollie lived here was such an ordinary one. It had to be someone distant, maybe someone from another part of the Harringtons' life, settling an old score or something."

"Susan, I love that you are our peacekeeper. But you're dreaming," Eleanor said. "There are a half dozen people within a mile of here who might have killed Ollie—and in their own twisted minds, had reason to do it."

"It's usually the spouse or guy next door. The one you least expect," Phoebe added enthusiastically. "Gus Schuette gave me a book to read on murder motives, and it's not complicated at all. It's pretty much for love or lust or money."

Kate laughed. "Phoebe, what are you reading books on murder for?"

"Someone has to solve this crime," Phoebe replied. "No offense against P.J. and his buds, Kate, but I don't see anyone being arrested. And if we don't clear this all up before Adele's grand opening next month, there will be no one making reservations in that bed and breakfast. And that means no one will see these works of art we're rushing to the finish line."

"The crime will be solved," Po said confidently. "And by the police, not us, not Kate or Phoebe rushing in to do heaven knows what." But deep down, Po didn't feel confident at all. Adele Harrington lived just a few blocks from her home, and the same distance from Kate's. Phoebe's apprehension was credible. Even when the trouble wasn't being talked about, it was there in the background of their lives—the awful fact that there might be someone in their midst who was capable of killing a kind, gentle man. And until that someone was found, the restlessness would remain.

"On a brighter spot, where's Maggie?" Eleanor asked.

"Don't know. And it's odd. I talked with her yesterday and she was definitely planning on being here to show off the progress on her quilt," Kate said. "Maybe there was a pet emergency."

Po frowned. "I hope that rattletrap truck of hers didn't break down on the way over."

Kate laughed. "I think Mags keeps that truck as a sign of her independence—snubbing her nose at that awful ex-husband of hers." A few years before, Maggie's then-husband had almost bankrupted her clinic, whittling away at her money on weekend junkets to Las Vegas. The truck was one of the few things Maggie didn't lose. But through hard work and with the help of good friends, she now had one of the most successful veterinary clinics in Kansas.

The sound of wheels on gravel in the alley behind the Elderberry shops broke into the conversation, and in the next minute, Maggie burst through the back door. But in place of the smile that almost always filled her round face was a disturbed look with brows pulled together and a clench to her square jaw.

"What's wrong?" Po asked.

Maggie plopped down on a chair and rested her elbows on her knees. "It's Emerson," she said.

"The poet?" Eleanor asked, handing Maggie a cup of coffee.

"Adele's dog," Po said, suddenly understanding Maggie's lateness. An emergency. "Is Emerson all right?"

"Someone tried to poison him," Maggie said.

Chapter 10

The quilting group disbanded shortly after hearing Maggie's news. The good news was that Emerson was going to be okay. But Maggie wasn't so sure about his owner. The vet was used to distraught dog lovers, but Adele, she told them, was deeply upset.

Po tried to move into the rest of her day but had trouble concentrating on much of anything. Her books lay stacked on the desk, unopened. Her computer silent. And the diminishing daylight cast a chill that even a cup of hot tea couldn't dispel.

A quick phone call to Max convinced him he needed to spend time on Po's deck that evening.

"First Oliver's death. And now a dog being poisoned. Max, what's going on here?" Po handed Max an icy martini, then wrapped a thick wool sweater around her shoulders and sat down next to him on the old wicker couch. She had repeated the story of Emerson's poisoning in full detail, down to the good news that Emerson would be returning home with Adele that night. "She wouldn't leave without him, and Maggie completely understood. She told Adele to call her any hour of the night if she noticed anything unusual with Emerson, and needed confirmation that he was going to be all right."

"Good for Maggie. And Adele can't be all bad. She really loves her dog." Max looked off into the deepening night. The flicker of small lights beneath the ancient trees cast shadows across the deep backyard. He stretched his legs out and sipped the martini. "It's not good, Po, that's for sure. I dropped some legal papers off for Adele on my way over but she didn't want to talk. Now I understand why. But Emerson will be fine."

Po nodded. She reached down and scratched Hoover's ears. Her ancient Irish setter thumped his tail in thanks.

"How did Adele seem to you?" Po asked.

"She was pure Adele. Always wanting to appear in command. But there's a softness there, no matter how hard she tries to hide it behind her accusations. She's convinced everything going on is 'evil doing,' as she put it. She tosses out names of suspects without a second thought. It's a long list, let me tell you. Everyone from Tom Adler, to neighbors, to the president of the College Board. People who want to scare her into leaving town."

"I know she's suspicious of Joe Bates, too, but that's probably just an excuse to urge him to find another place to live."

"Well, she can't force Joe out. It's in Oliver's will that he has a place there as long as he wants it. It was Adele's mother's wish as well."

"I'm glad to hear he's protected. But it can't be fun living where you're not welcome. And I know it irritates Adele. She doesn't much like being told what she can and can't do."

Max laughed. "That's putting it mildly, Po. She's got quite a temper."

Po took another sip of her martini and thought about Adele's life—or the little she knew of it. After college she'd followed her mother's suggestion and gotten a job with a pharmaceutical company, then traveled the world. By all accounts, she made plenty of money. Selma heard that she might have been married briefly, but no one knew for sure. And now here she was, back in Crestwood, Kansas, opening up a bed and breakfast. And turning neighbors and others against her with dizzying speed. Her life track didn't make logical sense, but then, sometimes that's how life was. "I think Adele might be all sound and fury," Po said.'

"Signifying nothing?"

"No. Maybe something. Perhaps a vulnerability—a fear of being hurt. If you push everyone away, no one is likely to hurt you."

"Well, it isn't working," Max said. "I think this thing with Emerson is hurting her."

Po nodded. Of course Adele was hurting, Max was right. "And there's Ollie. It's clear she loved her brother deeply." A breeze rustled through the branches and Po looked up beyond the trees, into a glorious fall sky. The stars were abundant, filling the black vastness with a brightness that belied the cloud hanging over Crestwood. She reached for Max's hand and felt his fingers comfortably wind through her own, icy now from the martini glass. But Max's was warm.

Warm and comforting.

He looked over at her and smiled. "Po, this mess will be solved, you know that. I know that. And soon, I suspect. Peace will return." Po rested her head on his shoulder. Yes, it would pass and the cloud would lift. The Harrington House at 210 Kingfish Drive would open to fine reviews. But between now and then, Po suspected life wouldn't be the same at all. And she wondered to herself how many lives would be touched in that interlude. The ringing of the telephone scattered her thoughts. She rose quickly, then paused. For a moment her heart beat too fast and she felt a fogginess inside her head. She stood still beside the couch, listening to the night sounds.

And for that instance, Po didn't want to answer the phone at all. The news, she knew instinctively, would not be good.

Chapter 11

Po walked into the kitchen and looked around the counter for her cell phone.

It was Kate, her voice higher than usual and her words coming out too quickly.

Po's heart skipped a beat. Since Kate's mother's death, Po had assumed that role with Kate that she had with her own three children—fearing, when the phone rings late at night, that a child might be hurt.

"Kate, what is it?"

"Oh, Po, when is this craziness going to end? P.J. and I were out on our bikes tonight, riding along the river toward the sushi place. Then—"

"Kate," Po stopped her, her knuckles white against the receiver. "Are you all right? P.J.?"

"Yes, yes," Kate said, impatient to get on with her story but having a hard time getting it out. "Everyone you love is fine. But there are others in Crestwood not so fine."

Po slowly released the air that was burning her lungs. "Go on, sweetie."

"We rode past the Harrington estate on the way back to my house, and as we were going around the corner, we heard sirens, then a police car, and then the emergency medical van spun around the corner and pulled into 210 Kingfish."

"Oh, Kate…"

"P.J. thought he could help, so we followed."

Po nodded into the still air.

"Adele Harrington was standing out in the driveway in her nightgown, though it was only nine or so. And Halley Peterson—that nice librarian from the college was there. And Joe Bates, the gardener."

"An odd threesome. Were they all okay? Why the police?"

Po could almost feel the adrenalin surging through Kate's body and wished, for a moment, that her goddaughter didn't love danger quite so much.

"Halley was in tears," Kate continued, "and Joe had blood streaming from his forehead."

"Good grief. That poor man. Is he all right?"

"It was mostly superficial, P.J. said. Apparently, Adele hit him with one of the workmen's tools because she thought he was breaking into her house. At least that's what she said."

"And Adele called the police?"

"No, Halley did. She was walking up the drive and heard Joe scream. Then she saw the blood as he was trying to get back to the carriage house. So she called 911 from her cell phone."

"What was she coming to see Adele for at that hour? That's so odd, especially since Adele isn't very fond of her." She felt Max standing close behind her and turned, assuring him with a smile and one hand raised that everything was okay. She nodded toward the coffee brewing on the counter and the apple pie beside it.

Max walked over and helped himself to a generous slice, then settled down at Po's table with Hoover at his side, listening as Po clicked the phone to 'speaker' mode.

"I don't know why Halley was there," Kate was saying. "Things were a little crazy, as you can imagine. Adele was upset that the police came. She said she could handle things herself."

"Did she bring charges against Joe?"

"No. She wanted everyone to go home and forget that the whole thing happened. Which they did, but of course the police had to file a report of the call."

"What happened then?"

"It was kind of anticlimactic. Adele went inside. Joe shuffled off to his carriage house with a bandaged head, and Halley kind of disappeared. I really don't know where she went.

"P.J. called in and talked to someone at the department for a few minutes—they thought the whole thing was weird. Adele's actions and the whole uncooperative way she's treated Ollie's death and murder have the police on alert. She isn't above suspicion, P.J. says. She only has the house because Ollie died. And things like this don't help the way they think about her."

"Surely Joe wasn't actually breaking in—"

"No. Why would he? And he has a key, so no, he wasn't exactly breaking in. Apparently, Adele heard a sound coming from the back door, picked up a hammer a workman had left, and clobbered him with it. She could have hurt him badly but somehow the hammer slipped in her hand. The paramedics checked him out, and they said he'd be okay."

"Adele doesn't like Joe, she's made that clear. But this isn't exactly the way to handle it. Why was he going into her kitchen?"

"He adopted Neptune, Ollie's cat, and he thought the cat had been locked inside the house. He didn't want the cat to have to spend the night with Adele, he said."

Po smiled. That sounded like Joe.

"I guess Joe mumbled something to the police about Ollie's murder. Said they were looking in all the wrong places."

"That's strange."

"He wasn't talking very sensibly. And everyone thought it was the wound and that he should go take some aspirin and go to bed. I think he'd had a few beers, too. He growled at Adele, then finally walked off. I had this feeling, I don't know..." Kate paused.

"What kind of feeling?"

"I don't know exactly, but for a moment, I felt sorry for Adele. She seemed vulnerable, standing out there on that driveway. She tried to put on her usual brave, brassy facade, but she couldn't quite pull it off. There was a crack in the stone."

A few minutes later, with Kate's assurance that she was through with any detective work for the night, she hung up and sat across from Max while he finished his own piece of pie and then hers. She filled him in on the pieces of the story he hadn't figured out from hearing one side of the conversation. The facts were unpleasant—and the thought of Adele swinging a hammer at old Joe Bates was an unforgiving one.

But beneath all the facts, Po suspected Kate was right. Adele's facade was crumbling. And she wasn't the ogre she wanted everyone to think she was. There was, indeed, a crack in the stone.

Chapter 12

Po had been trying to get to the Canterbury library for several days. Her excuse was to pick up another book Leah was holding for her and to do a little research. But the real reason was to talk to Halley Peterson again, to find out what in the world she was doing at the Harrington mansion late on a Saturday night.

A quick call to the library confirmed that Halley was working that day, and when Halley herself came to the phone, she agreed to meet Po for a cup of coffee around three. Po wasn't sure if she was reading into it or not, but she thought she heard relief in Halley's voice, or at the least, a desire to talk with Po.

Po threw a blue cotton sweater over her white blouse and jeans and walked the few blocks to the college. It was another amazing fall day with temperatures in the mid-sixties, and everywhere Po looked, trees were turning into bouquets of color. The ugliness of Oliver's death hanging over the town was an aberration and didn't fit at all with the beauty around them.

Soon, Po thought. *Please let it end soon.*

In ten minutes, Po reached the edge of campus and slowed down as she passed Eleanor's big house. Eleanor was like Joe Bates when it came to flowers, she thought as she paused to admire the large urns in front of the walkway. They were filled to overflowing with crimson mums.

A group of coeds in shorts and T-shirts came running by, and Po stepped aside, admiring their speed and energy as they ran toward town. Her own jogs were not nearly so speedy, now more of a brisk walk. But they energized her just the same. And also kept her in the same size jeans she'd worn years before.

Po walked beneath the large stone entrance arch and across the green quad that centered the college. She loved the campus and welcomed the flood of memories that warmed her from the inside out every time she walked the tree-lined lanes crisscrossing the campus. When Scott Paltrow had been president, Po stopped in often for one thing or another—to bring one of the kids by to see their dad, to have a little quiet time with her husband in his high-ceilinged office, to attend benefits and meetings. It was a second home, and Scott's early death hadn't changed that feeling. The faculty and staff considered her family and always made her feel welcome. Glancing over at a new all-glass building being built on the other side of the quad, she wondered how Scott would feel about the changes. Funding was an incentive, she knew, along with some semantics and the addition of masters' programs. But she resented the pressure it put on friends like Leah and Jed to publish articles and books if they wanted to remain in good standing.

Po greeted several faculty members as she walked past the theatre building and crossed over to the library on the other side of the quad. Inside the cool stone building, she was greeted by an enormous painting of her Scott, looking down at her from the paneled wall in the entryway. She nodded at him, smiling into his clear blue eyes. She let the catch in her breathing pass before moving on. Dear Scott. Always with her, but always, always, giving her permission to move on.

The library was busy with students cramming for exams. Po didn't see Halley behind the curved desk, but she was a bit early for their coffee date, so she headed for a computer to find her own titles.

A short while later, her yellow notepad filled with scribbles and two books checked out and slipped into her backpack, Po looked around for Halley. "Check the Hawthorne reading room," a young girl at the desk told her. "I think she was helping one of the professors with his reserved reading list."

Po thanked her and wound her way around a bank of carrels to a smaller room off a hallway. That room, too, was filled with students at library tables, heads bent together, books open between them, and a buzz in the air that spoke of pending exams.

Po spotted Halley over on the other side of the room, standing beside a carrel. She was talking softly to a man whose back was to Po. While she talked, she removed her glasses, then smiled shyly and leaned forward slightly to hear what the man was saying.

Po smiled as she watched the interaction. *She's flirting with him*, she thought with some surprise, then started to turn away, embarrassed to be eavesdropping on the librarian.

At that moment, Halley looked up and caught Po's eye. She gave her a small wave, said something to the man in the carrel, and hurried across the room, glancing up at the big clock on the wall.

"I'm so sorry, Po. I didn't realize the time."

"You were busy doing your job," Po said. "It's a little crazy around here."

"Yes," Halley said in a low voice. "Very crazy. Professors are trying to get reading lists lined up for the rest of the fall semester and the kids are cramming." With a sweep of her hand, she took in the crowded room. "Look at this, not an empty table in sight. But I love the activity."

Po noticed the sparkle in Halley's eyes, missing when she was talking with Adele Harrington just days ago. Her cheeks were pink and glowing. "I can see you love what you do," she said, and followed Halley's gaze around the room.

"Yes," Halley said softly. "I love what I do. I get to take classes for free, I meet fascinating people, and I work in this amazing library. This is where I met Ollie."

"You miss him," Po said, reading the wistful sound in Halley's voice.

"I do. And lots of others do, too. He had friends here, people who loved him."

Po nodded. "I'm learning that. And speaking of Ollie, shall we get that cup of coffee? I could use one. And we can talk more about your friend, too."

Halley agreed, and they began walking toward the door.

Po lifted her backpack over her shoulder and followed, glancing back briefly at the carrel in the back of the room and the man who seemed to have added a glow to Halley's cheeks.

The man was getting up, closing his briefcase, and turned briefly to speak to a student asking his help.

Po smiled in surprise as she looked at the handsome profile of Jedson Fellers. Goodness, she thought, one never knew.

"A cup of coffee is exactly what I need to keep me going another couple of hours," Halley said as she and Po settled in a booth in the small coffee shop that the college had recently constructed. It was a light and airy place with comfortable couches and chairs and a line of booths along one window.

"How long have you worked at Canterbury, Halley?" Po asked.

"Forever, it seems." Halley pushed a strand of loose brown hair behind her ear. "Long enough that I still call it Canterbury College." She laughed.

"After a few years in the library, I started taking classes, so now I combine the two. The work, of course, makes the other possible—and the college is very generous to its employees."

Po nodded. Halley Peterson was a hard worker, which she suspected from the first time she saw her—a hard worker and a woman of purpose. Just going back to school when you were in your mid-thirties took some gumption. "And you and Ollie became friends here, you said."

"Yes, we did."

Halley's face was a mirror of her soul, Po thought as she watched a range of emotions spread out from her eyes. Sorrow, colored with happy memories. Po understood the blend well.

"Ollie spent lots of time in the library when he wasn't in classes. Sometimes new students poked fun at him—he was so much older than they were and his social skills with the younger crowd were a little backward. But before long they stopped the teasing because so many of us knew him and liked him, and once you talked to him, you saw the kindness in him. Professors let him sit in on classes, and he knew everyone. Professor Fellers, especially, took Ollie under his wing. But you probably know that. Jed was a mentor to Ollie, and then they became good friends." Halley paused and took a drink of coffee. For a moment, she and Po sat in silence with the memories of Ollie Harrington filling the space between them.

Halley wrapped her long fingers around her coffee cup and lifted her head, her eyes on Po. "Sometimes Jed and Ollie invited me to join them when they were talking about astrology, and a couple of times the three of us went down to the Powell observatory in Louisburg for a Saturday night program. Ollie didn't go out much, but he loved going down there with the professor. Jed would explain to us what we were seeing, and then we'd go somewhere for coffee and talk about it all. Ollie would get so excited. He learned so much from Jed, and Jed would just sit there and beam at his prize student, so proud as Ollie waxed eloquently about all those things—the Pleiades cluster, the Andromeda galaxy, things I'd never heard about before."

"I didn't know about that part of Ollie's life. It makes me happy to know he had special times with good friends."

Halley wiped the moisture from her eyes with the back of her hand. "Ollie loved those times, and he loved being here at Canterbury," she said. "He used to tell me that Canterbury was his surrogate family. And when I met his sister, I understood why he said that."

"You aren't fond of Adele," Po said.

"I don't know her that well," Halley answered, a slight trace of defensiveness in her voice.

"But you've talked, that I know."

"That was foolish of me. Sometimes I get involved where I don't belong. But I cared so much for him. Ollie even convinced me to take a class in astronomy last semester."

"From Jed?"

Halley blushed slightly. "Well, Ollie told me he was the best. And he was right."

"It's good Ollie's friends have each other now. That helps. I know when my husband died, my friends at Canterbury were so important."

"Jed was mostly Ollie's friend. But since Ollie's death, we share lots of good memories. It's good to have someone to talk to, you know? I can tell him how sad I feel and he understands. I told him it would mean a lot to me to have something of Ollie's. He suggested I talk to Adele. And I was also upset about other things...so I went to see her."

"He had a beautiful telescope..." And it was clearly valuable. Adele might well be put off by someone wanting to take it. It might even be grounds for the anger they had witnessed.

Halley responded quickly. "Oh, no, not that. Absolutely not. Telescopes you can *buy*, Po. I wanted to get some of Ollie's writings, some of his thoughts that he put in written form. Some books. Even books he might have written in." She looked out the window, as if deciding how much to say to Po. When she turned back, her words were deliberate and careful. "Once in a while Ollie would talk about me sharing his home someday." Halley paused for a long time. When she spoke again, her voice was profoundly sad. "And then he was murdered. I knew he didn't just die. I tried to tell Adele. But no one would listen."

"The police are doing everything they can, Halley."

"Then why is Adele Harrington still building a bed and breakfast? Why is she still occupying that house, acting like everything's fine?"

"Do you think Adele had something to do with Ollie's death?" Po asked. A young waitress appeared and refilled their cups, then disappeared across the room.

"It's the only way she could get her hands on that property. I know Ollie wasn't going to will it to her. Adele never liked Crestwood—Ollie told me that. She doesn't deserve his home—he wanted someone to have it who would appreciate it."

"Someone like you."

"Or Joe Bates, or anyone who would care for it, not turn it into a way to make money."

"I heard what happened to Joe Bates the other night."

Halley's head shot up. "You know about that?"

"I do—"

"Of course you do. Kate Simpson was there. And her boyfriend. Standing in the distance. I almost forgot."

"Why were you going to see Adele again? Was it for his writings?"

Halley laughed softly, but it wasn't a humorous laugh. "I wasn't there to see her. I was there to check on Joe."

"Joe? Was he getting something in the house for you?" That would explain a lot of things. Perhaps Joe was the one who had entered the house a few nights ago, looking for things of Ollie's so they wouldn't be thrown away.

She shook her head. "No, Joe wasn't breaking into her house. He wouldn't do that. He was just trying to get Neptune, like he told the police. Neptune was Ollie's cat, and he sometimes went back into the house, looking for Ollie. I had just arrived when it happened.

"Joe is terribly lonely now, and every now and then he calls me and asks me to come look through the telescope with him like he and Ollie did. Or look through some of Ollie's things that he'd confiscated from the trash pile that Adele was throwing out. He'd go through it every single day to be sure nothing of Ollie's was heaved into the dumpster.

"But the other night he was very upset when he called. He said I needed to come talk to him. He knew who killed Ollie, he said, and he could prove it if only I would help him find something."

Po frowned. "Find something?"

Halley smiled sadly. "Joe has been a little crazy since Ollie died. He didn't always make sense. He's been obsessed with things, first about the house, who would get it. And lately about things that weren't always logical. The other night he was particularly anxious, so I thought I would go talk to him and make sure he was all right."

"So you think he was just ranting? Do you think he really has information about Ollie's death?"

"I don't know, Po. He loved Ollie so much, and he hasn't been himself since this happened. I think sometimes he feels guilty, like he should have kept Ollie from dying."

"That's a burden he shouldn't have to bear. Joe has been with the family for a long time. Whenever I went to see Ollie, Joe would check me out, make sure he knew who I was. He was probably the best security guard Ollie could have had, not that he needed one. Joe rarely left the property since Mrs. Harrington died. I asked him once if he'd do some more yard work for me, and he told me he couldn't—his job was with Oliver. Ollie couldn't have asked for a more devoted friend."

Halley listened carefully and then looked out the window again. Students wandered by alone and in groups, enjoying the fall sunshine. Taking a break from midterms. Finally, she pulled her attention back to Po. "Joe and Ollie were an odd couple—Ollie the brain, Joe the caretaker. Ollie said his mom made sure that Joe was always there for him."

"And Ollie's father? Did he ever talk about him?" Po had known Walter Harrington socially, but had always found him slightly unapproachable. Distant.

"No, he didn't talk much about his father. I don't think Mr. Harrington had much to do with his son. He wasn't mean or anything. Just not very present to his son. Ollie wasn't going to take over the family holdings or be the corporate leader his father was, so he didn't matter much, is the way I interpreted it. It was his mother Ollie cared about and who cared about him."

"I know when she was diagnosed with cancer a couple of years after Walter died, Ollie was bereft."

"He told me about that. Ollie was about my age when she died, I think."

Po nodded. "About that, maybe a little older. Ollie became kind of a recluse for a while, then sought out the college, and he seemed to find a life again."

"It's all so tragic. This sweet man. There was a brilliance beneath his simple surface, at least when it came to constellations and things like that."

Po smiled. That was so true. She remembered how as a young boy, Ollie would come to her door, selling odds and ends he'd find around town so he could buy small binoculars or books about the stars. He'd tell her exactly where Mars was that day and what his favorite constellation was. And he was so happy when someone would listen to him.

"Why would anyone kill Ollie?" Halley asked suddenly. "Is land that important? Did Adele want that house so badly? Or the developers? Or even the college? Enough to kill him? In the four years I've known Ollie, Adele visited him once. Once! And it wasn't pleasant—I think she loved her brother, but she thought she knew what was best for him, what would make him happy, and ignored what he really loved. She wanted Ollie to move into a small condominium near her and sell the house. Can you imagine Ollie in a condominium? It was an awful time for him. And now she's back and has what she wants. The estate is all hers. And she's turning it into something he wouldn't have liked at all."

"Maybe he'd have liked his sister coming home, Halley," Po said gently. Tears ran down Halley's cheeks, and she looked away, embarrassed. "Do you really think Adele was involved, Halley? Maybe it's your deep sadness in losing a friend and wanting some resolution to that."

Halley looked back at Po. She dabbed at her eyes with a napkin, then shrugged her narrow shoulders. "Somebody killed Ollie," was all she answered.

Po reached across the table and covered Halley's hand with her own. "Yes, someone did that terrible thing. And someone will pay for it—and hopefully that will be soon."

* * * *

Much later that night, Po stood in her robe on the back porch steps, looking up at the same sky Ollie Harrington respected and loved with great passion. Replaying her conversation with Halley Peterson, she wondered about her own hollow words. Halley was lashing out at Adele because there was no one else to focus on. Ollie's sister was the visible sign of the loss Halley had suffered in losing her friend.

But the thought of Adele killing her own brother didn't fit easily in Po's mind, not any more than it did when she'd first heard the rumor.

A breeze whipped her robe about her legs and she stepped back inside, closing the screen door behind her. It was unsettling: her conversation with Halley, and even more, the uncomfortable feeling that there were secrets at 210 Kingfish Drive that threatened people she knew. A feeling of dread was building up in the neighborhood—a lovely neighborhood where people wanted to live, a street where she walked alone at night, safely, unafraid. Having that lifestyle threatened was disturbing, unsettling, and in the end, it made Po angry. She walked inside and put a kettle on to brew some tea before bed. It would be hard to sleep.

Halley might be right. Sometimes it seemed like no one was doing anything.

Chapter 13

Joe Bates shuffled around the side of the wide garage and walked toward the pond in the back of the big house. The sun was slowly climbing above the trees in the east and he could feel the soft early morning glow on his leathered skin.

It'll be a chilly day, he suspected. A fall day tinged with impending winter. He clutched the thermos of coffee and planted one foot after another, drinking in the morning air. Not that the days had all been so great lately, but early morning seemed to escape the plight that affected the rest of the day. It was his special time, another world, and he could forget for a while the things that had gone bad, the dark days and the dangers all around him.

It was still quiet at this hour, before the jostling groups of foul-mouthed workers invaded his home. They'd come today, even on a Saturday, he knew. No peace. But for this brief hour, it was just Joe and his pond and the soft flat lilies floating along the surface. But no Ollie, who used to bring him blueberry muffins that he'd make all by himself. They'd sit beside the pond and watch the last remnants of the galaxies fade into the light of day.

Ollie would go on and on and on about those planets and stars that were so real to him they nearly became family. Lordy, how Joe missed that boy. Loved Ollie like a son, quirks and all. He was a good boy. Not sharp-tongued like that sister of his. Not cruel like his father. Kind and gentle, just like his sweet mother, God bless her soul.

The thought of Oliver gripped Joe fiercely, and he paused on the flagstone pathway, his head cloudy and sad. Then, with the commitment he'd made to Ollie, he continued on toward his pond, trying to push the painful thoughts aside. Old Missus Harrington had left it up to him to watch over Ollie—even gave him the apartment up behind the garage so he'd stay close. And what'd he done? Let him get killed. And now he'd have to do something about it. Bring honor back to the boy. And now at last he knew how to do it. He'd right the wrong. Just like the Bible told him to do. Joe settled down on one of the boulders that ringed the lily pond. He remembered when they had lifted those rocks in place years and years ago. Brought in a huge old crane and dropped them right in place. Directed it himself. Joe carefully unscrewed the top of his thermos and felt the steam rise up his nose, wetting the thin hairs.

He hadn't understood Oliver's ranting at first. Ollie'd been so mad, he didn't make much sense. The boy didn't get mad much, but this time he thought he'd lost not just what was his, but a part of his soul, he told Joe. People had given him the short end of the stick often. He knew that and had learned not to care. But this time it was dead wrong. They couldn't take it away from him. He wouldn't let it happen.

Joe hadn't quite understood. He had thought Ollie was talking off the top of his head like he sometimes did about the stars. Mostly he had wanted to calm Ollie down, to let him know he'd always be there. But finally Joe understood. And finally he had the proof he needed to make it right. He'd show the high and mighty Adele Harrington the way it was, sure as he knew his name was Joe Bates.

Joe leaned forward, staring into the water, cleaned by the dozens of koi that swam in slow circles just beneath the surface. Soon his boy would rest in peace. Joe bowed his head and briefly removed the faded Royals cap from his head. With gnarled fingers, he made a sign of the cross over his chest. *Requiescat in pace.* It was the least he could do for his Ollie.

He squeezed his eyes shut and wrapped his arms around his body, shivering now, and he prayed all the way up to the heavens that he'd have the strength to do this one last thing for his boy. He slipped the cap back over his thinning white hair.

With his eyes closed, Joe didn't see the shadow fall across the pond. And with his hearing not so perfect anymore, he missed the quiet sound of shoes across the path, missed the lifting of the large stone rock behind his back, up in the air over his head.

He didn't see, nor did he hear. He felt only the rush of air as the large rock crushed down, unforgiving, on the top of his head.

For a brief second, Joe saw the lilies and the fish look up at him. Spread apart. Welcome him.

And then all was black, and Joe's body folded over and rolled off the rock as gracefully as a seal that was finished sunning himself. With nary a sound, he slipped beneath the cool, soothing water of his pond.

Requiescat in pace.

Chapter 14

Maggie's new van was parked at the curb, directly in front of Selma's store. She stood on the sidewalk beside it, beaming. "Okay, ladies," she said, "this may be your only chance to ride in my new chariot before it's full of dog hair, tools, and dings."

"Mags, it's beautiful," Kate said, admiring the shiny white van with "Helmers Pet Care" painted along the side in bright blue swirling letters.

"Thanks." Maggie put her hands on her hips, her eyes bright. "I'm keeping the truck for old times' sake—but isn't this a hunk? And before I take out a row for cages, it will nicely fit all eight of us, I do believe." She slid open the big side door to reveal three rows of seats.

"Very nice, Maggie," Po said. "It's about time you got something for yourself. And it's a vast improvement from that rusty truck, beloved or not."

"Let's get this show on the road," Selma said. "I want to be back before the early Saturday morning crowd comes in and drives my staff crazy."

"Selma, don't fret so," Susan said. "Things will be fine. You need to start taking some time off, away from the store."

"And realize that it really will survive without you," Leah chimed in.

Selma waved off their words and pulled herself up into the van, puffing a little as she settled herself near the window. "Hand me my bag, will you?" she asked Phoebe, who slid over next to Selma.

"Very cool, Maggie." Phoebe reached over and helped Eleanor up into the van.

Kate, Leah, and Susan slipped around the settled bodies into the wide third seat, Po joined Maggie in the front, and in minutes the Quilters were off, heading down Elderberry Road toward the Harrington mansion.

"Why do you suppose Adele wanted us all to come?" Maggie called back over her shoulder. "You'd think looking at quilts on the beds would be the last thing she'd be thinking about."

Po shifted on the seat. "I think she's just wanting some assurance that something in her planning is going right and is under her control. She seemed jittery yesterday when I talked to her."

"Very jittery," Kate piped up from the back of the van. "And a little paranoid. She stopped me yesterday as I was biking by the house—she was pulling out of the drive in that long Cadillac of hers—and wanted to know if I had seen anyone suspicious in the neighborhood. I felt kinda sorry for her."

"This is an enormous undertaking for her," Po said. "Max said it's costing more than she had anticipated."

"Well, that's the way of the world," Selma said, looking out the window.

"Maybe we can cheer her up a bit," Leah said. "I think our quilt tops are beautiful."

"Of course they are!" Phoebe said.

"And we're here," Maggie announced, pulling into the driveway.

"This is the first time in days I've been able to see all the way back to the carriage house," Po said as Maggie pulled over to the side of the drive. "Not a truck in sight."

"But there will be," Selma said. "The renovation crew is here seven days a week, old Mrs. Porter tells me. She said she can hear the commotion all the way from her house on the corner. She's ready to spit fire at Adele. Her husband patrols the street, just waiting for something to go wrong."

"The Porters have a bone to pick," Eleanor said. "A truck ran over their new chrysanthemum bed. She explained it to all of us in the supermarket. The lettuce practically wilted beneath her tirade. Unhappy neighbors are not a good thing."

Po was half listening, wondering about Joe Bates and the clobbering he'd taken. Maybe she'd try to find him before they left. "It's good we've gotten here earlier before the workers," she said. "Shall we get this over with?" She opened the door and began walking toward the house.

The front door opened before they reached it. Adele stood just inside, waiting for them.

"You're prompt, as always," Adele said, holding open the door. "I like that. Thank you for coming."

"Like I haven't been dying to see the inside of this place?" Phoebe answered. She touched Adele on the arm and smiled brightly. "This is amazing, Adele. I want to see every single inch of it."

Po noticed the instinctive tightening of Adele's muscles at Phoebe's light touch. The poor woman probably isn't touched much. The thought made Po sad.

"I thought we would go directly to the guest rooms and lay each quilt on a bed so I can get a feeling for how they fit in," Adele said. She led the group of women carrying their quilt tops up the wide, winding staircase to the second floor. Her back was rod straight, and her face unreadable.

"Maybe my sweet Emma will get married here," Phoebe whispered to Kate, her small hand sliding along the walnut banister.

"Phoebe, she's three years old."

"Well, one needs to plan." Phoebe grinned, then lifted her chin up into the air, imagining herself walking alongside her daughter.

At the top, Adele waved the quilters into separate rooms, directing them to smooth their tops out on the beds.

Po walked down the hallway and into the small room that had been Oliver's. Everything was the same as the last time she had seen it—the book case filled with books, the small desk positioned beneath the window with a yellow pad of paper and cup of pencils ready for his use. She stretched out her quilt on the narrow bed and stood back.

"It's perfect," Adele said from the doorway.

Po turned. "Do you think Ollie would have approved?"

Adele nodded. Her smile was sad.

"This must be difficult for you," Po said.

"I don't let things be difficult, Po. It's a choice."

"Not always. But you do seem to handle things that would get the better of most of us. At least on the outside they are being handled."

Adele didn't answer. She walked over to the window and stood next to Oliver's telescope, aimed up to the sky. Po walked over to her side.

"I didn't neglect my brother, you know." Adele's voice was so soft Po could barely hear her words. "I did the best I could under the circumstances. Things are not always as they seem."

Po felt an urge to wrap an arm around her, to pull her close and comfort her. To let her feel a warm body caring for her own. But she knew instinctively the slight crack Adele had allowed to open would close in a heartbeat if she disrupted the moment.

Adele looked back at the quilt, and when she spoke this time, the softness was gone and the protective shield was back in place. "The colors are good and the paint color goes well with it, don't you think?"

Po nodded. She looked around the room and agreed that the deep blue of the walls and the wide white molding were perfect for the multi-starred quilt. And then her gaze settled on Ollie's desk and the yellow pad, waiting to be used. "Ollie didn't use a computer, I guess. But he loved to write. I can't imagine writing anything in longhand anymore."

"He wrote all the time, even when he was little. It was one thing he could do well. It was his best way to communicate. Some people are like that, you know."

"I understand that. Especially people who take more time to process what they want to say. I sometimes feel that in my own writing."

"He wanted to write a book someday. That Peterson girl wanted all his writings, but I wouldn't give them to her. Why would I do that?" Adele shook her head and bent over to smooth the quilt with the flat of her hand. "Everyone wants a piece of Ollie," she said softly.

"People liked him, Adele," Po said. "Their reasons are honorable."

Adele didn't answer, but the slight nod of her head told Po that she knew it to be true. And she wondered if for Adele, giving away Ollie's things was losing some of Ollie all over again.

"Here you two are," Selma said, walking into the room. "I think all the quilts are going to work beautifully, Adele."

Adele turned around. "You've done a nice job in an impossible amount of time. Once they're completely finished, we'll have an open house so everyone can see. And now we will have coffee and scones down on the back veranda before you leave."

"No need for that," Selma began, but Adele had already walked out into the hallway and toward the steps, motioning for everyone to gather their quilt tops and follow her.

"I guess we'll have coffee and scones," Selma said to Po, shrugging her shoulders. "But let's keep it short, Po. I have a full day ahead of me."

"We all do, Selma. I agree. Short it will be."

The wrought iron table on the brick veranda was set with an embroidered tablecloth. A platter of blueberry scones sat in the center, next to a vase of bright yellow mums and pot of sweet butter. Adele urged them to make themselves comfortable and walked back inside to get the coffee.

"This is lovely," Po said, admiring the tasteful setting. She walked over to the railing that bordered the veranda and stood next to Kate.

"It's nearly perfect," Kate said, looking out over the yard. Sunlight streamed through the trees, casting soft shadows across the recently mowed grass.

"This backyard is awesome," Phoebe said, coming up beside them. "So cool! If we put in a slide and wading pool, maybe a zip line for when they're older, it would be a perfect park for Emma and Jude."

"There's a pond down beyond that clump of trees," Kate said, pointing to the flagstone path that led to Joe's pond. "Much better than a wading pool, Phoebs. The gardener tends to it so lovingly you'd think Monet was going to show up to paint lilies any day,"

"Can we see it," Phoebe said. She looked back toward the French doors. "Let's go look. Adele is still inside."

"She'd probably be happy to have it admired," Po said.

The three women walked along the winding path to the pond, bordered in hardy boxwoods. Miniature cherry trees and small gardens of ornamental kale and sea oats waved at them along the path.

Po slowed and touched a colored leaf tip on a low-hanging Japanese maple branch. "I came out here a few times with Oliver and Joe to walk around the pond—it was lovely then, but now the plantings are so green and lush and filled with foliage that you can barely see the pond."

"It'll be a magical place next spring when all the hydrangeas and dogwoods bloom," Kate said. "I think you're right, Phoebs. It's the ideal spot for a wedding."

Phoebe lifted a brow and looked up at Kate. "But let's not wait for Emma..."

Kate laughed.

"Do you know something I don't, Phoebe?" Po looked over at Kate, one brow lifted.

Kate ignored her and walked ahead.

"I think I love it here," Phoebe said, walking around a shade grove of hydrangeas that circled a clump of towering pine trees. "It really is a park."

"I wonder if Joe is around today. You'd like him, Phoebe," Po said. "I don't want to come upon him suddenly and frighten him, though. His hearing isn't very good."

She stopped on the path and looked back toward the garage.

Kate and Phoebe walked on, rounding a granite boulder that allowed them a full view of the pond.

"Po," Kate spun around and called out, her voice urgent. "Come fast."

Po rushed around the curve just as Kate and Phoebe neared the edge of the pond.

"Look," Kate said when Po reached her side.

She followed the point of Kate's finger toward the distant side of the pond where a clump of lilies fanned out, separating from one another. A faded blue KC Royals cap floated between the leaves. On the shore just beyond it, lying beside a rock, was an abandoned thermos.

Po stared down into the water. And as the lilies moved in the chilly breeze, she spotted the cause of the urgency in Kate's voice. The blue ball cap moved slowly away, and beneath it, a school of brilliantly colored koi swam in and out of the waving strands of Joe Bates's thinning white hair.

Chapter 15

Going to Marla's Bakery and Café Sunday morning with Leah Sarandon was a tradition as old as Po and Leah's friendship, and it was in keeping with that tradition and nothing else that found the two women sitting in the busy bakery the day after finding Joe Bates's body.

Po looked around at the nearly full breakfast spot. The line was beginning to form outside the windows and would soon be winding down Elderberry Road, people coming from church or home or a college dorm.

"Bad news brings people out," Leah said. "I guess they want answers. But gossip is such a bad place to look for them." She sat back as a young waitress put an omelet down in front of her.

"It's so ugly," Po said, the images of finding Joe's body still tightly wrapped around her heart.

Adele had spotted them out at the pond and walked down, mildly irritated that they weren't sitting at the patio table. And then her face changed, the blood draining out and her eyes focused on the lily pads, the cap floating among them. On the grisly sight in her beautiful backyard.

Phoebe and Kate helped her back into the house, though she tried to shrug them off. Po stayed behind, calling the ambulance and the police from her cell phone.

She stood alone at the lily pond, feeling a need to protect Joe until help came. To not leave him all alone. To talk to him, hoping his spirit was hovering around her, listening.

Within minutes the driveway was once again filled with spinning blue lights and the kind of attention no new business would wish upon itself. After the quilters were questioned by the police, they left, except for Po and Kate, who urged Adele to rest. The asked if they could contact any of Joe's relatives.

But there were no relatives, Adele had told them. That much she knew about the old man. And then she had collected herself, looked out at the garage and carriage house, and announced that she'd now need to do some renovating of the apartment. It could be a suite—perhaps for honeymooners. Po had cringed, grateful no policeman was around at the time. Sometimes Adele was her own worst enemy. And sometimes shock did strange things to people.

Po shook off her thoughts and looked up into the unsmiling face of Marla Patrick. "I wondered if you two would show up," she said, a slight scolding tone carrying her words. Her brow was dotted with perspiration as she leaned over the small table near the window. "Who would have imagined that skinny woman had it in her?"

"What are you talking about, Marla?" But Po knew the answer. Marla had already convicted Adele Harrington. And that meant there were many others in the room uttering that sentiment. Marla's opinions were often formed—and usually fueled—by her customers.

"Adele Harrington, that's who. She did old Joe in as sure as I'm breathing. I knew she was up to no good soon as she came back to this town." Marla straightened up and scanned the room. Then she continued in a lower voice. "Tom Adler's over there. He said that he was over at the house the other day and heard Adele say she wanted to get rid of old Joe."

"Tom isn't too fond of Adele, Marla," Leah said.

"Tom hates her, sure. He would love the place to fail, and then he'd scoop it up himself. But that doesn't matter one whit. What matters is that the Harrington woman will stop at nothing to make things go her way."

"You don't know that," Po said. "And talking about it that way doesn't help anyone."

"I know what I know," Marla said, maintaining her stance. Her small green eyes moved from one woman to the next. "I don't like to speak ill of anyone any more than the next one, but the town is filling up with bad vibes. I can feel it. It's going to affect business, too. We need all out-of-town folks to keep coming to Elderberry Road and they'll stop coming if this evil cloud hangs around much longer. Adele Harrington needs to be put in jail or driven out of town."

Driven out of town. The words lingered uncomfortably in Po's head, reminding her of articles she'd written about the early days of quilting. It often was the way of dealing with people not wanted in a town all those years ago. *Drive them out.* And often it was what folks did. Cruelly and unfairly.

She shivered and looked over at Tom and his wife. He was standing now, handing his wife her sweater and collecting his bill. He would certainly like the B&B to fail. But to kill for it?

Po watched him talking with his wife, then walking to the next table and greeting the mayor. Could Tom possibly have done something as awful as drown poor Joe Bates to make Adele look bad? To try and to run her out of town? Was her peaceful town turning into a vigilante community?

None of it made sense. But Marla was right about one thing—the activities at 210 Kingfish Drive needed to stop now, before any more damage was done.

"Po?" Leah said. "Marla has moved on. You can come out of your cocoon."

"Sorry. I'm trying to piece some of this together, but it's impossible. It's like piecing a quilt with shapes that don't match."

Leah agreed. "Adele may not be the most lovable person in town but I think Marla is wrong about her. Besides, you don't kill someone just to get them off your property. A sheriff can do that."

Po moved her eggs around on the plate. She and Leah were of like mind. But no matter how you looked at it, things were not looking good for Adele.

"Am I interrupting?"

Po and Leah looked up into the swollen eyes of Halley Peterson.

"Oh, Halley," Po said. She took Halley's hand and pressed it lightly. "I am so sorry about Joe."

Halley shook her head.

And then they saw that Halley wasn't alone. Jed Fellers walked up behind her and gently rested one hand on her shoulder. He nodded to Po and Leah. His face was drawn, his eyes troubled. "Not the best of days, is it?"

"No, it's most definitely not," Po said.

"Halley called me about Joe as soon as she heard," Jed said. "It's all over town. Not too many people knew Joe, but it doesn't matter. It's affected everyone. But especially those of us who knew Ollie—and knew what an important person Joe was in his life."

"I couldn't stay in my apartment," Halley said. "I wanted to scream or beat on someone or be sick. Jed suggested a walk instead."

"Halley was probably one of the few people in Joe's life since Ollie's death," Jed said.

"I saw how he greeted you that day," Po said. "Joe didn't let many people into his life. I think you were one of the few."

Halley managed a sad smile. "He and I had been spending more time together since Ollie died, going through the few writings and things of Ollie's that Joe was able to wrest from Adele or dig out of the trash. He was such a good man." Her voice broke. "He certainly didn't deserve to have his life end like this."

"No one deserves something like this, Halley," Leah said.

Po watched Jed as he motioned to a waitress and ordered tea and scones for Halley. She was grateful that the librarian had someone to lean on. Dealing with Ollie's death, and now having another tragedy touch her life, must be nearly unbearable. A slight blush had colored Halley's cheeks when she looked at Jed, and his returning smile was comforting. Po wondered if it was more than friendship. They seemed an unlikely couple, but the difference in age seemed to fall away in the looks they exchanged. And Jed was certainly a very young fifty. Something lovely in the middle of all this sordidness would be a good thing for everyone.

"Do you know if there will be a service for Joe?" Halley asked. "I know he doesn't have family. I'd like to do something if I could. I wanted to call Adele, but she doesn't like me very much—"

"I'll try to find out, and I'll let you know," Po said. "I'd like to help, too."

"I could pack up his things, too. I don't want Adele throwing them out—" She looked up at Jed.

He agreed and offered to help her. "Adele probably doesn't want to be bothered with it. And from what Halley tells me, she and Joe didn't much like each other. But I know Ollie liked him. He used to talk about Joe often."

Po agreed that Adele might not want to be bothered. But she also knew that she didn't like strangers on her property, and Po doubted if Halley and Jed's kind offer would be received well. It was a shame, because Halley would treat his belongings with respect. Adele would most likely shovel everything into a dumpster.

Halley sensed her hesitation. "I know, she probably won't want me meddling. But it's worth a try. I'm going to ask anyway."

Leah finished the last trace of her eggs and sat back, her napkin beside her plate. "On a happier note, congratulations again on the book, Jed. I hear it's receiving good reviews. A feather in your cap. Or your cap and gown I should say."

Jed smiled awkwardly. "I guess you could say that."

Leah looked over at Po. "Jed is being modest. The chancellor has offered him the department chair."

"Good for you, Jed. You certainly deserve it," Po said. She remembered those tense days when Scott was a young professor, needing that affirmation from the college administration. Well, this was good. And they needed good news these days.

Jed seemed uncomfortable with the attention and soon had turned the conversation back to Po and the quilters, asking about their quilts for 210 Kingfish Drive.

"Almost finished," Po said. "We're working on borders and backs now, and then they'll be quilted by a wonderful lady over in Parkville. It's been a nice project, except for all the grisly goings on over at the Harrington place."

Po placed a bill down on top of the check and pushed out her chair.

"How about you two take our table before Marla gives it away," Leah said.

Po gave Halley a hug, then turned and followed Leah toward the front door. "Let's make a getaway before Marla heaps more gossip on our shoulders," Po said softly into Leah's ear. "She means well, I suppose—"

"Or not," Leah laughed. She pushed open the door, and Po followed her out into the bright cool sunshine of the fall day.

Po started to walk down the street when Leah grabbed her arm. "Po, look." She pointed across the street.

Po turned back and followed Leah's nod.

Tom Adler stood across the street next to a pear tree, bending low and staring through the closed car window of Adele Harrington's empty Cadillac. He straightened up and scanned the block, looking both ways.

Just then, a figure emerged from Max Elliot's law office a few doors down. Adele Harrington, dressed in a bright blue silk suit, walked down the office steps and headed toward her car. Sunday walkers passed her by, a few nodding a hello, others casting curious, suspicious looks. Adele seemed to ignore them all, her head held high and her eyes cast straight ahead.

Po and Leah watched as Tom stepped away and moved behind a shade tree. hidden from Adele's sight.

She removed her keys from her purse and for a minute it appeared Tom was going to step forward and say something to Adele. But then a horn honked and Tom's wife waved to him from a bright red BMW parked a few spaces back. Tom lowered his head, turned, and hurried to his car.

Chapter 16

Po and Leah watched Adele's car pull away from the curve and head down Elderberry Road, taking the corner fast enough to scatter leaves in all directions.

"What's that about?" Po asked.

Leah shrugged. "Beats me. I'm glad Tom's wife had the good sense to remind him not to do anything dumb."

"I wonder what Adele was doing at Max's office on a Sunday morning." Po shifted her purse on her shoulder and she and Leah began walking down the street toward Gus Schuette's bookstore.

"With all that's going on at her home, she probably needed some legal advice."

Po had had the same thought, and Max would meet someone in need in the middle of the night if they asked. She glanced over at the small brick building that housed his office and noticed his car was gone. He'd clearly come in just to solve Adele's problem, whatever that might have been. She'd probably see him later, but Max was a paradigm of discretion and wouldn't bring it up. But that certainly had never stopped Po from asking.

They reached Gus's bookstore and walked into the comfort of books and soft music.

Po's shoulders seemed to loosen the minute she walked through the door. Gus had modeled it after an old bookstore he visited in London—hardwood floors, paintings placed on available wall space, and lots of small rooms crammed with shelves and library ladders and overstuffed chairs begging to be used. She loved it all, and the owners, too. Gus and Rita Schuette had been in her life longer than she could remember. Scott used to tell Gus that he and Po had singlehandedly paid for the Schuette kids' education with the money spent in the store.

"Hey there," Gus called out from a chair behind the wooden checkout counter. His glasses hovered low on a wide, misshapen nose. He stood, his face breaking into a grin. "My Sunday ladies, here at last. Let the day begin." He automatically reached beneath the counter for two reserved copies of the Sunday *New York Times*. He handed them across the counter. "I could set my clock by you two."

"You say that every single Sunday, Gus," Po said.

"Sure I do. What would we do without our rituals, Po?"

Po smiled. Gus was right. The familiarity of routines and dear people were what Crestwood was all about. She and Leah had started the Sunday routine years ago, when Leah was a brand-new professor at Canterbury College. Scott Paltrow soon discovered his new faculty member's husband loved Sunday morning golf as much as he did. So while Scott and Tim swung clubs, Po and Leah, the sixteen years between them melting away in a flash of an eye, began their Sunday morning walks to Elderberry Road for Marla's eggs or waffles, for talk and friendship, and always, for a quick trip to Gus's store for the *Times*.

"Kate was in soon as the doors opened." Gus looked over his shoulder and nodded toward a side reading room. "She and P.J. are in the back, sitting on the floor with a stack of books in front of them, just like when they were kids."

"Except he isn't pulling her ponytail like he used to."

Gus laughed and waved as the "kids," as he called them, walked out of the side room, their arms loaded with books. They were dressed in jeans and turtlenecks, windbreakers wrapped around their waists, their faces flushed and water bottles hanging from belt buckles.

"Early morning bike ride," Leah called out.

Kate laughed. "You got it. It's all those mysteries you read, Leah."

"Looks like you two are supporting Gus's retirement."

"It's only right." Gus grinned at Kate. "Lord knows you gave me enough trouble when you were a kid. Always reading. Never buying. Glad to see things have changed a little."

Kate punched his arm lightly. "You're all talk, Gus Schuette. You loved our trouble." She turned toward Po and Leah. "So what's the word at Marla's? P.J. and I tacitly agreed to stay far away." Kate's face grew serious with the question.

P.J. looped an arm over Kate's shoulder. "Have they figured it all out over there?"

"Most of the talk was about Adele and Joe's contentious relationship. At least that's the nice version," Leah said.

P.J. frowned. "Yeah. Adele doesn't do herself any favors. A lot of people heard her talking about Joe, criticizing him, wanting him off her property."

"But it's all anecdotal," Kate broke in.

"That's my line, Simpson. You're starting to talk like a cop. Cool it." Kate laughed.

"Don't know why anybody'd want to murder that old man," Gus said.

"Did you know him?" Leah asked. "Joe was such a recluse, most people only knew him by reputation."

"Except for people our age," Po said. "In his youth, Joe was the person we all went to when grass wouldn't grow or we needed the best ground cover or our dogwoods weren't blooming. I don't think there's a home in my neighborhood that hasn't been touched by Joe Bates."

"He was smitten with Mrs. Harrington, I think," Gus said. "Absolutely devoted to her."

"I remember that, too. After a while, he only worked for her, staying in the garage apartment, and that's when we didn't see much of him anymore."

Gus rang up Kate's books and handed her the receipt. "I was surprised when Joe came in here recently. Almost didn't recognize the fellow, been so long since I'd seen him."

"Joe was here?" Po asked.

"Just a few days ago. Wanted me to order him a book. I tried to get him to stay awhile, to catch up on things. But he wasn't having it. I showed him some new garden books but even those couldn't convince him to hang around. I watched him through the window when he left, trudging back down the street, toward 210 Kingfish Drive, I suppose. His head was down, his face all pinched together in sadness. He seemed determined, kind of, like he had things to do, but you could see that Ollie's death had taken a toll on him. Wiped him out."

"Maybe he was finally trying to move beyond the Harrington House—to begin a life without Ollie," Kate said.

"Maybe." Gus scratched his square chin. "Maybe so. He was, well, a little agitated. But I hadn't seen him for so long that I figured maybe that was his normal look as he'd aged."

Po frowned. Joe had been agitated the last time she saw him, too. But for good reason. Adele was wanting to evict him and surely he felt that pressure. Aloud she said, "Joe was a good sort. His murder is troubling and senseless. It's awful for the whole town, but above all, for Adele Harrington.

Having someone murdered in her backyard isn't going to help promote her bed and breakfast any."

"Some folks think it might have been an accident. Adele has quite a temper. Maybe she just meant to shake him up," Gus offered.

"I'm afraid there'll be a lot of 'maybes' floating around," P.J. said. "And they will only hurt Adele."

"Does all this speculation hurt the case, P.J.?" Kate asked.

P.J. shrugged. "I'm not on the case, as you know. But from what I can tell, probably not. The investigation will go forward on its own course. But what speculation does is hurt innocent people."

"Like Adele. I don't know what it is about that woman—she's insulted so many people—but there's more to her than that," Kate said. "When Phoebe and I helped her into the house yesterday after those awful moments at the lily pond, we could see genuine agony in her eyes. Real, sincere hurt. She mumbled something we couldn't quite understand, something about her mother. And Ollie. And how horrible this would have been for them both."

"I've seen traces of that, too. There's something real and decent there," Po said.

"Well, it wouldn't hurt the woman to let a few others see that side of her," Gus said. "Rita and I invited her to a book signing here at the store—one of those cocktail things we do. We thought maybe she'd like getting to know some folks—"

"And maybe fill her B&B library from books she'd buy here?" Leah teased.

"Sure, a little business. A little pleasure. But you know my Rita, she decided this is what a newcomer in town needs and she would have introduced her to everyone within fifty miles."

"But she turned you down," Kate said.

"Flatter than Kansas," Gus said. "And was rude in the process."

"It's a protection, I think," Po said. "But in time she'll warm up."

"Well, let's hope she's not finding herself warming up in the cooler."

Po shook her head. "You're hopeless, Gus, and on that note, I need to get moving. We're going to stop by Adele's to see if there's anything we can do."

But when Po and Leah drove down Kingfish Drive a few minutes later, they could see that the iron gates leading to the drive were closed, and in the distance, crowding the curve of the drive, three police cars stood guard over a murder scene.

* * * *

That Sunday night, P.J. and Kate, as they'd been doing lately, showed up first for dinner, followed closely by the others. Po had tried to reach Halley, thinking she might need company, but when no one answered, she left a voice message.

P.J. offered to man the grill while Kate prepared drinks, and Po urged the others out to the patio near the grill to enjoy the wonderful starry evening, maybe the last outdoor gathering before winter set in.

"I got a strange call today," Maggie said, standing near the grill as she watched P.J. line up shrimp and vegetable kabobs on the grate. She wore faded jeans and a soft fleece jacket. "Adele Harrington called me at home. She asked me to open the clinic so she could bring Emerson in to board him." Maggie eyed the platter of Thai spring rolls that Eleanor was passing around. "Isn't that kind of weird? Emerson seems to be her one true friend—you'd think she would want to keep him close, especially at times like this."

Eleanor pushed up the sleeves of her silky red blouse and handed Maggie a small plate with a spoonful of peanut sauce for the spring rolls. "Yes, that's odd," she said. "Adele loves that dog more than life itself. I ran into her down at the river park the other day while my yoga class was doing its thing on the lawn. She looked like she hadn't slept in a few days, but every time Emerson rubbed against her, her face relaxed and she seemed almost happy."

"Seems like Adele placed more than one call this morning." Leah looked over at Max. He was standing beneath a tree, throwing a Frisbee for Hoover, his face thoughtful. He turned as Leah called his name.

"Po and I saw Adele leaving your office bright and early today."

Max took the chilled martini Kate handed him. "This is a difficult time for her," he said. "But the meeting wasn't anything unusual or private. We were checking some insurance policies to make sure the property was covered."

"That sounds ominous," Maggie said. "Isn't that something you do before you die—or go off to jail?"

Po listened to the conversation as she walked back and forth between the house and the group standing around the grill. The night was so pleasant she'd decided they would settle into the comfortable lawn chairs and eat right there beneath the stars. An unconscious tribute to Ollie Harrington, perhaps. And possibly a reason why she should have invited Adele. But she knew before the thought settled that Adele wouldn't have come. Were she in Adele's situation right now, socializing would be the last thing on her mind, no matter if she'd be among friendly faces.

"Did Adele talk about Joe's funeral at all?" P.J. asked. "They won't release the body for a couple days, but someone should be making plans to give the guy a decent burial or memorial."

"No. I asked, but she ignored me on that one," Max said. "I don't think she feels responsible for burying Joe, and I suppose, officially, she isn't."

"Jed Fellers and Halley offered to help," Po said. She put a basket of napkins and flatware on an old picnic table beneath the tree.

"Reverend Gottrey offered to put something together, too," Leah said. "It's sad when there's no family—or even close friends—to take care of these things."

P.J. carried a platter of skewers stacked with plump, spicy grilled shrimp and scallops to the table. Po followed with orzo sprinkled with feta cheese, a basket of sour dough rolls, and a heaping bowl of spinach salad.

"Please, help yourself," she said, slipping on a thick cardigan sweater. "It's good to be with friends. While that's always true, sometimes it matters even more."

Beside her, Max nodded. He looked up at the stars flung wide across the black sky. "This sky makes me think of Ollie. He was so brilliant when it came to the heavens."

Po smiled. Ollie was touching them all tonight.

P.J. and Kate were sitting together on an old rope hammock that Scott had given Po for Mother's Day decades ago. The ropes, weathered to a pale gray, groaned as P.J. leaned back, ignoring the roll that slid off his plate onto Kate's lap. He looked up. "It's a great sky. I imagine both of them up there, Joe too, wondering about all this chaos below."

"I never met either of them, and that's so odd in a small town like this," Maggie said.

"I think you had to fit into a certain compartment in Ollie's life," Leah said. "Otherwise your paths wouldn't cross. Ollie's life seemed to be the college, his classes and talks with Jed, the library. And Joe's was with Ollie and his gardens."

"Don't forget Halley Peterson," Po said. "It's somehow comforting to me to know that Ollie had a friend like her. And it's clear she genuinely cared for him. And for Joe, too. The past couple weeks have been miserable for her."

"P.J. and I ran into her today after we left Gus's store." Kate pulled herself out of the hammock and walked her empty plate over to the table. She grabbed a sweater from the back of a chair and returned to the hammock.

"She and Jed were walking toward campus, deep in conversation. I don't think they even saw us. Halley looked upset, and so sad. Jed was clearly being a comforting shoulder to lean on."

"They have Ollie in common. I'm glad Halley has someone to talk with. As busy as Jed is, he's making time for her, and that's a good thing," Leah said.

"Coffee anyone?" Po asked, rising from her chair.

"And I brought ice cream," Eleanor added. "Let me help, Po."

As the two women headed inside, the sound of a siren in the distance cut through the crisp night air. Eleanor paused at the porch door. "Such a mournful sound," she said. "And it always means distressing news for someone."

Po looked out into the darkness. Tiny lights illuminated the giant trees in her backyard—a perfect, peaceful setting. But she felt it, too, the unsettling feeling of unknown lives being changed in an instant by an auto crash, a heart attack, a random, freak accident. Po held open the screen door and followed Eleanor into the house. "Let's hope it's no one we know, El."

Eleanor busied herself in the kitchen, scooping large portions of ice cream in bowls while Po filled a tray with cups, cream and sugar, and a full thermos. "Fudge sauce?" Po asked.

But before she could open the refrigerator, a different sound, much closer, joined the sirens.

"Now that's a sound you don't often hear," Eleanor said, wiping her hands on a towel and glancing toward Po's front hall. "It's your doorbell. Who in heaven's name uses your doorbell, Po?"

"Not many people," Po admitted. "Not when they know it's just as easy to push it open and walk in." Po walked quickly toward the front of her house. The sound of the sirens quickened her step as she reached the front door and pulled it open.

Po looked outside, but before she could speak, Halley Peterson flung herself into Po's arms.

Chapter 17

"Oh, Halley, dear," Po murmured, drawing the disheveled woman into the front hall. Her hair was loose and messy, falling over her shoulders. A sweater was wrapped carelessly around her shoulders and her Canterbury T-shirt was half-tucked into the waist of her jeans. For a brief moment, Po thought she might have been in an accident. "What is it, Halley? Are you all right?"

Halley drew apart, wiping away the tears that streamed down her cheeks. She nodded, her throat tight.

"Come in," Po said, and drew Halley through the entryway and into the warm glow of the family room lights. Eleanor brought a glass of water over while Po urged Halley to sit on the couch. In the distance, the sirens increased in volume, filling the night air with a strident symphony.

Kate rushed in from outside, her dark hair flying. "Po," she called out, "there's a fire somewhere. We can smell the smoke." She stopped suddenly, spotting Halley.

"It's Joe—" Halley said, looking up at Kate.

"Joe?" Po asked gently. The wild look in Halley's eyes was disturbing. And now her words weren't making sense.

Halley shook her head, as if trying to straighten her thoughts, to put them in order. "Joe's apartment," Halley said. Her voice was almost a whisper. "The Harrington's garage is on fire."

By then the rest of the Sunday supper crowd had come inside and were busying themselves in the kitchen, putting dishes in the dishwasher, talking softly, and hoping Halley could provide more information as they listened to the voices across the room.

"Were you there?" Po said, sitting beside the distraught woman.

Halley nodded. "Jed and I went over to see if Adele would let me into Joe's place. To...to get some things he and I had looked at together. The police were gone by then—it was late this afternoon—and I knew Adele wouldn't wait long to throw everything out of Joe's apartment. I wanted to salvage some things Ollie had given Joe, some things that meant a lot to him. She almost threw me off the property, threatened to call the police. Said she'd had enough bad things happen to her. And then...then she seemed to weaken. And she told me she couldn't deal with anything right then. She was exhausted and would be going to bed early. But she said I could come back tomorrow."

Po handed Halley a tissue.

"But I wasn't sure she meant it. I didn't trust her. So I went back late tonight by myself, determined to not let all remnants of those two good men end in a dumpster. I figured she'd be asleep." A sad smile eased the tense lines outlining her face. "I knew where Joe kept a key to his place, and I decided I'd just go in and take some things. I know it's wrong, but I didn't care. I walked along the bushes hidden from the house, and was halfway there when I spotted the flames."

"And then?"

"And then I was so frightened that I turned and ran in the opposite direction, back toward the street. I didn't want Adele to see me. And then I..." Halley paused and seemed to be deciding what to say next. When she spoke again, her words were planned, thoughtful, careful. "Then I wandered around the neighborhood for a while, away from the Harrington house but close enough to hear the sirens, not knowing where to go. I had heard your message earlier—"

A knock on the back door broke into the quiet room.

Max walked over to it and pushed it open for Jed Fellers, his face washed in worry. "Halley? Is she here?"

Max nodded and motioned for Jed to come in. "She's in need of friends, I think," he said softly and motioned toward the living area.

Jed smiled his thanks and walked over to the couch. He looked at Halley's tear-stained face. "Are you okay? I was so worried when I got your message. I could hear those sirens all the way over on campus—but I couldn't find you."

Halley wiped the tears from her cheek and looked up at Jed. "Jed, it was so awful. I know you told me not to go over there, that Adele would turn me away. But I had to—"

Po got up to make room for Jed on the couch. She walked over to Max while Halley repeated the story to a distraught Jed.

"Po," Max whispered, "P.J. and I are going to run over and check on Adele. We'll be back shortly."

Po nodded.

"Adele was home," Halley was saying now. "Standing in the driveway, watching it burn. I saw her—"

And she probably saw you, Po thought, trying to put the distressing consequences out of her mind. She sat down across from Halley and listened while she finished telling Jed how she'd run away, frightened and unsure of what to do.

Eleanor had put on a pot of tea and placed a cup down in front of Halley, along with a jigger of brandy. "This will warm you, dear," she said. "Jed, I think I'll bring you a stiff drink."

Halley took a sip of the tea. "I didn't mean to interrupt your dinner. I just, well, I knew Jed was busy tonight and I didn't know where else to go. And it was all so awful, seeing those flames."

"Po's door is always open, Halley," Leah said. "You made a good choice. And you're not interrupting anything. This is exactly where you should be."

Jed took the drink that Eleanor handed him and smiled his thanks. "Scott's suppers pulled me through some lonely times in the past. This would have been a safer place for Halley to be tonight, that's for sure." He looped an arm around the couch behind her. "Halley was just trying to help with Joe's things. But I don't think Adele can let other people in yet, not even to help."

"She's starting to let her defenses down a little, but you're right, Jed," Po said. "It's going to take her awhile." Po could see the color coming back into Halley's cheeks as they talked.

"I know I shouldn't have gone over there," Halley said, her voice stronger now. "Jed warned me. But I only wish I'd gone sooner,"

"You and Ollie were very close," Kate said.

Halley nodded. "I loved him. Not in a romantic, get-married kind of way. But we had a kind of spiritual connection," she said. "We read to each other and wrote poems together. We shared our thoughts. I've never been able to do that with anyone before. Ollie was different. And he knew I appreciated that he was different and didn't condemn him for it. He did the same for me."

The sound of the back door slamming announced that Max was back. He poured himself a cup of coffee and joined them near the fireplace. "It's under control," he said. "P.J. stayed on to talk with the police."

"Police?" Po said.

Max hesitated, then said, "The fire wasn't an accident."

The room was silent.

"They're sure?" Po asked.

Halley's eyes filled her oval face. One hand covered her mouth. Jed's arm dropped to her shoulder and he pulled her into his side.

"Yes, they're sure," Max said. "It was definitely arson. But only Joe's apartment was affected. The garage below wasn't badly damaged. Whoever did it wasn't very adept at lighting fires if the goal was to burn the whole estate down. The breezeway leading to the house was only mildly burned."

"How is Adele?" Eleanor asked.

Max was quiet for a moment. He wrapped his fingers around the warm mug of coffee. When he spoke, he chose his words carefully. "Adele was upset, just as you'd expect her to be. A murder in her backyard and a fire within one single weekend is enough to shake the most stalwart of folks."

Po listened. She couldn't imagine what Adele must be feeling right now. She wondered if this might be the final straw. Would Adele call it quits, sell the property, and move away to another life that didn't include murder and fires and someone threatening her dog? She suspected it's what most of them would do.

Max placed his mug on the old coffee table that filled the space between the two overstuffed sofas. "Halley, this isn't what you need tonight, but I need to tell you something."

Halley pressed closer into Jed's side, but she looked directly into Max's eyes.

Po could tell that Halley wasn't going to be surprised at what Max would say, though she was dreading the words.

"Adele told the police that she saw a woman running away from the garage," he said. "She didn't name you. But she described you, from your brown hair, down to your Canterbury T-shirt."

Halley's eyes were dry now, her face composed, and her look level and direct. "And I saw Adele, Max," she said. "I saw her standing in the driveway as straight as an arrow, calmly staring up at the flames lapping at the side of the carriage house. That's what I saw."

Chapter 18

It was Phoebe who called the impromptu quilting gathering for Monday night. The emails went out first thing Monday morning and the tone was insistent.

Meet at Selma's at seven tonight. Bring your quilt, your spirit, and your desire to turn our town back into a safe place for my babies!

Po wasn't sure if it was Phoebe's dismay at missing the excitement of Sunday night that precipitated her action, or simply her big heart and desire to help Halley Peterson out of the mess she'd fallen in to.

But she knew it was more than her desire to put the finishing stitches on Adele Harrington's quilts.

The quilters worked better with food, so Kate brought a fettuccini salad with fresh dill, and crisp grilled vegetables, sprinkled with Romano cheese. Po brought leftover apple pie, and Eleanor brought two chilled bottles of pinot grigio. While Selma plugged in the coffee pot, Po gave an abbreviated account of the fire.

"So poor Halley is under suspicion now?" she asked when Po was finished.

"Yes, but poor Halley is a strong woman under her vulnerable façade. I suspect her life hasn't always been easy. By the time she and Jed left my house, she was composed and ready to let the police know that she was the woman Adele spotted running away—but that she had absolutely nothing to do with the fire." Po pushed her glasses up into her hair and began taking finished blocks out of her soft carrying case. "P.J. thought that was best, and he and Max are both going to the station with her this morning."

"The thought of Halley trying to burn down Adele's home is crazy," Maggie said. "What possible reason would she have for doing that?" Maggie positioned her cutting mat, picked up her rotary cutter, and began slicing through strips of bright blue fabric for her binding.

"Be sure to use double bias binding for these quilts," Selma said, taking a pin out of her mouth. "They're going to be used a lot and will hold up better."

Phoebe looked with dismay at the single binding she had begun to stitch on her quilt.

"No problem, Phoebe dear," Selma said. "But the crib quilt will especially need it because it will get lots of washings. We can fix that in a jiffy." She took the quilt from Phoebe's hands.

Leah poured herself a cup of coffee and sat down next to Maggie. The thick oak table was filled with strips of binding materials in a multitude of colors. Most of the tops for the B&B quilts, as the group called them, were ready for their bindings. "The talk at the college today was all about the fire and Joe's murder. Parents are calling, wondering if there's a psycho on the loose. 210 Kingfish Drive is too close to the campus for comfort."

"It's too close to all of us for comfort," Po said. "I'm beginning to wonder if it's safe to walk at night, and I've never felt that way before in all the years I've lived in Crestwood."

"Are there any leads?" Phoebe asked. She looked around the group.

All heads turned toward Kate. As P.J.'s soul mate, she sometimes had news the papers hadn't latched onto yet, but soon would. P.J. had become adept at ignoring questions Kate shouldn't be asking.

Kate stood near the back window, coffee in her hand as she tried hard not to dribble it on her crisp white blouse. The lights from the lampposts lit streaks of red in her thick hair. She ran her fingers through it now. "I don't think so. At least none that P.J. has been willing to share with me. He can be obnoxiously stubborn sometimes. But I know he's worried because of what it's doing to the town—and to the people involved. The longer this festers, the more damage it does to people's lives."

"We need to do something. This bed and breakfast is the future home of our quilts, ladies," Phoebe said, pushing back her chair and rising to her full 4 feet 10 inches. "What are we going to do about it?"

Kate laughed at Phoebe's pronouncement, but admitted that she was absolutely right. "P.J. said arson cases are often helped along by people calling in tips, things they saw that night. But geez, I don't think tips are worth waiting for."

Susan walked over to the iron and began pressing a binding strip. "The bad thing is that Halley was the person seen leaving the garage. The news interviewed several neighbors—it was such a nice night that even though it was late, a few people were sitting out on their porches. The person they described seeing sounded like Halley. Apparently, she wandered around the neighborhood after leaving Adele's."

"But if I hadn't been at Po's, it could have been me they saw," Kate said. "I walk through that neighborhood all the time. This is a walking town—" She put her cup down and gathered her hair in one hand, impatiently pulling an elastic hair band around it, as if her unruly hair was somehow to blame. "Halley didn't try to burn that house down. I'm just sure of that."

"But she was over there, trying to get inside. Why?" Phoebe asked.

Po listened and realized she'd been wondering the same thing. She hadn't slept easily, thoughts of the burning garage and images of Joe's body still burdening her thoughts. Halley's reason for going over to Joe's was logical enough on the surface, but something about it didn't sit right. Breaking into someone's home, even if you had a key, was a serious thing. And Halley was a smart woman. And even Jed had warned her against it, someone you'd think she'd have listened to. And he had promised to go back with her the next day.

A thought came to her and she turned to Maggie. "Didn't you say Emerson stayed at the clinic last night?"

"Yes. I was just about to jump in. Adele came to the clinic today to pick him up. Now that's plenty weird, don't you think? That she boarded her dog the day of the fire? Then picked him up the day after? What was that about?"

There was silence, as eight minds pondered Adele's action. As hard as she tried, Po couldn't come up with a logical explanation. Emerson was the only thing Adele seemed to care about. The one thing she would want to protect in case of a fire.

"But why would she set fire to her own house?" Leah asked.

"Maybe there was some incriminating evidence against her in Joe's things," Phoebe offered.

"But she lives there, for heaven's sake," Eleanor said. "She owns all of it. All she had to do was go up in the apartment and find whatever she wanted and destroy it."

There was silence as they all sorted through the conflicting motives and actions.

Selma walked over to the sideboard and filled a bowl with Kate's pasta. "Sorry, friends, I can't wait. I'm starving." She sat down in an old rocking chair near the food table. "Adele came in here today after she picked up Emerson. She asked how the quilts were coming. But that wasn't why she really came in."

Po looked over at Selma. "No, I don't suspect it was."

The two of them and Eleanor were the only ones who knew Adele in more than a very casual way. And without discussing it, she knew Selma was thinking the same thing. Adele needed someone to talk to.

"She didn't say much, of course," Selma went on. "That's her way. But she wanted to talk, I could tell. She looked terribly sad, but couldn't express it or ask for help. Adele is so self-contained that letting someone in just might cause all that glass around her to shatter."

That was Po's perception, too. And yes, so terribly sad. What would she have done without friends and shoulders to lean on when Scott had died? And all the days since, when things went wrong or bad things happened to good people. Many, many times. Her life would be barren without her friends to bring warmth and color and love to it.

"This pasta is great, Kate," Maggie said, standing near the table. "Selma, I had that same feeling about Adele when she came into the clinic. She looked truly sad today. Not guilty. Not mad. Just sad. She was even nice to the office staff. I had this urge to ask her if she wanted to go get a beer."

"Well, the truth of it is, emotions are one thing, but we have to be logical about it," Phoebe said, grabbing a pad of paper from the old secretary Selma used to do her paperwork. "We know in our hearts she didn't do all these awful things, or at least we think she didn't. But okay, everyone, think this through with me." Phoebe began scribbling on the paper:

Adele—motive.

Susan looked up. "With Ollie gone, Adele inherited the house," Susan said. "That's motive for killing Ollie. And she had said in front of all of us that she wanted Joe gone."

"But the will gave him the right to stay," Po said.

"So, motive for getting rid of him," Phoebe wrote.

"But the fire. Why the fire?" Selma asked. "That doesn't make sense."

"Insurance money?" Maggie said.

"Of course!" Phoebe said, her fingers moving across the paper. "Mags, you're super smart. She will have money to redo the carriage house now."

And the remodeling money was running low, Po thought.

That much Max had shared with her the night before. Adele was worried because she wanted the bed and breakfast to be absolutely perfect. But Po kept her thoughts to herself. There was enough on Phoebe's pad already to condemn the poor woman. Could she possibly have killed her own flesh and blood? The thought caused tiny goose bumps to climb her arms. She rubbed them lightly, forcing the moment to pass.

"Okay," Phoebe said. "Moving on—Tom Adler. We know he thinks Ollie was going to let him have first bids on buying 210 Kingfish Drive when he died. Tom's business is in deep trouble, so my Jimmy tells me. Tom's glamorous wife is a friend—no make that protégé—of Jimmy's mom, and she told me that the Adlers had to give up their membership in the Crestwood Country Club last month." Phoebe laughed at the thought, a light, delicious ripple that she couldn't hold in.

"Phoebe, shame on you," Kate said, smiling at her friend and knowing that Phoebe would like nothing better than to relinquish her membership in the Crestwood Country Club. All the quilters knew Phoebe's relationship with her wealthy mother-in-law was a precarious one. Though she tried to get along with her because she knew the older Mellons genuinely loved their grandchildren, Phoebe—a former bartender—didn't fit comfortably into their elegant lifestyle.

Phoebe shook her short platinum hair. "No, all's I'm saying is that Tom's pretty wife really likes her house and jewelry and all the things she's gotten used to. And Tom is nuts about her, Meredith says, and he'll stop at nothing to keep her happy."

"*Stop-at-nothing*—write that down, Phoebe," Maggie ordered.

"Okay. But what about Joe Bates? And the fire?" Phoebe asked.

"I suppose different people could have done these things, but it doesn't seem likely," Po said.

Eleanor sat up straight and looked around. "Maybe it was as callous as this: Joe's murder and the fire, and, God forbid, whatever awful thing comes next, are intended to make Adele's business fail and drive her out of town."

"Leaving the property free for Adler's company to develop," Maggie finished.

Phoebe wrote furiously.

"And then there's Halley Peterson," Kate said. "Poor Halley, thrown right into the middle of all this."

"But she doesn't seem so innocent, maybe, when you look at the facts," Maggie said. "Apparently Halley was also told the house would be hers someday. Ollie liked her very much, you all have said. Let's suppose he had told her she was in his will

"Well, okay," Po said. "But she would never kill Joe."

"How do you know, Po? All you know about her relationship with Joe is what she's told you. Did she really like the guy? Who knows? She clearly wanted something from him, she admitted that herself," Maggie said.

"I don't think she did it either. But she was seen running away from the burning garage," Leah said. "That's not good. And none of us can quite buy her intense desire to get into that apartment for sentimental reasons. What was that all about?"

Phoebe stepped in. "And, she didn't much care for Adele, that we do know. Maybe she thought Adele killed Ollie and was getting even? Burning the place down would certainly accomplish that." Phoebe's words tumbled out.

She looked over at Po and noticed the deep frown lining her forehead. Phoebe waved a hand through the air. "Oh, Po, we all like Halley. I met her the other day in the library when they had a reading hour for kids, and she was so sweet to Jude and Emma. People that nice to my kids don't kill people. This is all hypothetical. We have to put everything down." She looked over at Eleanor. "El, I think we all need to have a glass of your wine—"

"There are also people at the college who wanted that property every bit as badly as Tom Adler did," Leah said. "Who knows what kinds of deals they had tried to work out with Oliver? I know for a fact he had made an appointment to see the chancellor—I was in the office when he came in and made it, and if I'm not mistaken, it was set up for the very day after he was murdered."

Leah pinched her brows together as she searched back in her memory. "Yes, I'm positive it was that day, now that I think about it. Ollie was agitated and seemed distracted when I tried to talk to him. It was unlike him. Something was clearly on his mind and he seemed disturbed that the chancellor couldn't talk to him right at that moment. His secretary calmed him down and promised she would get him in first thing the next day."

"And then, that night he died. Before he ever got a chance to talk to the chancellor. Maybe there actually was an agreement with the college regarding the house, and he was going to cancel it." Leah was talking about her own college family now, and her voice was soft and unconvincing.

Po accepted a glass of wine from Eleanor. The timing was suspicious, but from what Po knew of Ollie, he could have been meeting with the chancellor for something else, something very minor. Little things sometimes agitated Ollie, like computers that didn't work or classes that got cancelled. And he wouldn't have hesitated to go to the highest authority he could think of to solve the problem. But what if it *was* something important? But maybe it had nothing to do with his house. "Phoebe," she said aloud, "we need to be careful with all this. These are terrible things that have happened. And even being hypothetical like this puts us in a certain amount of danger."

Po was looking at her goddaughter as she spoke. Kate and Phoebe were sometimes double trouble when trying to protect someone they liked or when they thought things were moving too slowly. Their actions were born of generous spirits, but they worried her nevertheless. Moreover, she'd vowed to Kate's mother before she died that she'd watch over her daughter, no matter what. Kate's free spirit made that difficult sometimes.

"Po, I can read your thoughts," Kate said softly, coming up beside her godmother. She put a hand on Po's shoulder and squeezed it slightly. "You have P.J. on your side, too, you know, and he warns me to mind my own business every chance he gets."

Po nodded and sipped her wine. Kate's words were sincere. But at the other end of the room, Phoebe was printing their hypothesizing on an erase-board that Selma used for teaching. And Po knew she wouldn't be able to relax completely until the murderer was found and the board was filled instead with diagrams of how to match up patterns. She wanted the innocent to be able to get on with their lives.

And she wanted those she loved to be safe.

Chapter 19

Po's Tuesday calendar was filled to the brim. And the only way to approach a day filled with errands and book research and a conference call with her publisher was to get up early and hit the road with a nice slow run—or a brisk walk, whichever way it went.

She lifted her legs over the side of the bed and stretched out the sleep that had settled in her joints. In minutes she had pulled on bright green stretchy pants and a Trolley Run T-shirt, downed a glass of orange juice, and with Hoover at her side, headed down the shady street.

Po loved this time of day, but early as it was, the streets weren't empty. Canterbury coeds were out in full swing and passing her frequently with polite, indulgent nods, reminding Po of the speed of bodies several generations younger than her own.

Undeterred, Po continued her comfortable pace through the winding leaf-strewn streets that wrapped around the college. Hoover happily ran beside her. As she neared the Kingfish Drive intersection, she took an unplanned turn and headed down the long shady street that housed the Harrington mansion. She would tell Eleanor later that she hadn't planned that route. But something, somehow, pulled her to the wide gated entrance of 210 Kingfish Drive. Hoover was the one who spotted the form on the driveway. And in that instant, both Po and Hoover heard a frantic barking. In a flash, Hoover was gone, racing up the long Harrington driveway. Po followed quickly, calling to Hoover to stop.

But instinct reigned over command, and in seconds Hoover stood near the figure of Adele Harrington, crumpled up beside the steps leading to the charred carriage house apartment. Emerson stood beside her, vigilant, and keeping Hoover at a respectable distance with a low growl.

"Adele!" Po reached her a minute later and crouched down beside her. "What happened? Are you all right?"

Adele was grasping her ankle, her face white and shadowed with pain.

"Oh, Po," she began, an artificial bravado forced into her voice. And in the next instant, the always composed body of Adele Harrington collapsed into sobs. Emerson wedged his way in between Po and Adele and began licking his master's face.

Po rubbed the dog's head, then wrapped her arms around Adele's shaking shoulders and held her while tears ran down her cheeks. Finally, the sobs subsided, and Adele reached for the tissue Po had pulled from her pocket. "What a fool I am," she said softly.

"Your ankle is swelling, Adele. Let me help you into the house."

"Thank you," she said and allowed Po to reach beneath her arms and help her to an upright position. "I fell, you see. I was having trouble sleeping, so Emerson and I took an early walk around the grounds." She hobbled beside Po to the back door leading into the kitchen.

Po braced Adele as she pushed open the door and helped her inside. Emerson and Hoover, their sniffing of one another complete, followed.

Po pulled a chair from the table and carefully settled Adele on the cushioned seat, then pulled out another for her throbbing foot.

"Now, let's see if I can remember my first aid training," Po said, grabbing a stack of towels from the counter and positioning Adele's injured ankle on the soft cushion. Gently she moved her ankle to make sure there was nothing broken, then carefully pressed the skin around her foot.

Adele, with Emerson's head resting in her lap, wiggled her toes. "I don't think there's anything broken," she said.

"I don't either. But you have a nasty sprain. Sometimes that's worse."

Po went to the sink, poured Adele a glass of water and spotted a bottle of acetaminophen on the windowsill. She handed two small pills to Adele. "Take these for now—it will help the pain, and I'll run you over to the emergency room when it has settled down some."

Adele shook her head. "Not necessary, Po. I can tell it's a sprain. There's nothing you can do."

Po found a bowl in the cupboard and filled it with ice from the freezer, while Adele directed her to an ice bag in the butler's pantry. Po filled it, wrapped it in a towel, and gently placed it on her ankle.

"Did you trip on something, Adele?"

Adele took a drink of water and set the glass down on the table. Perspiration dotted her brow. She wiped it away with the back of her hand and sighed. "It was silly. I looked up at the carriage house as I was walking with Emerson and realized I was going to have to go in there at some point to see what could be salvaged. So Emerson and I started up the stairs. But I tripped and fell. Clumsy. Foolish."

"Neither of those. But certainly unfortunate."

Adele reached for a tissue from a box on the table. She dabbed at her eyes. "Thank you. It was nice of you to stop."

Po smiled. "You can thank Hoover. He spotted you as we were going by."

"You run in the morning, Po? I used to run, when I lived back east."

"You should start again." Po looked at her ankle. "Well, maybe not for a while but when you're feeling better. I'll stop by someday, and we can run or walk together. It's beautiful down by the river early in the morning."

Adele looked at her carefully, her eyes clearing. "Why are you being so kind to me? I haven't been very nice to you. Not to any of you."

"It's not calculated, Adele. After all that's happened lately, you are probably suspicious of anyone who speaks to you."

Adele managed a slight laugh. "And anyone I speak to is suspicious of me. Or worse. I know what people think, Po."

"People are frightened, that's all. We're a quiet town, peaceful neighborhoods. And anything that disrupts our lives makes people nervous and wary. It's the curse and blessing of small-town living."

"How could anyone think I'd kill my twin brother?" she asked suddenly.

Po shook her head. "I don't know, Adele. But you swept down on us so suddenly, took over this house. People don't know what to think."

"And what do you think, Po?" Adele's shoulders stiffened with the question. She looked directly into Po's eyes.

"I don't think you killed Ollie, Adele. Not for a minute. And I don't think you killed Joe Bates or set fire to that garage, though you've given people reason to believe you might harm Joe."

"That's nonsense." Adele's voice became stronger as she spoke. But the familiar edge was softened. "Joe Bates and I never got along. Even when I was a child. He loved Ollie and he loved my mother, but I was always a nuisance to him. He watched over Ollie—my mother charged him with his care—and that was a good thing. But when I came back and Ollie was gone, but Joe was still here. Along with all those memories. I was resentful, I think. Irrationally so, perhaps. And I took out my frustration on him. But God knows I didn't kill him."

Adele lowered her head as her eyes filled.

"Maybe I resented him for doing what I didn't do—come back here to help Ollie after my mother died. All those things. Seeing him every day made it worse."

"Well, he did a good job of caring for Ollie, so you can take solace in that. He was a good friend to him."

"I think he understood him better than I ever did."

The sound of a truck on the driveway broke into their conversation, and Po rose to look out the window. "Workmen," she said to Adele.

"Yes," Adele answered.

Po watched as she took another drink of water, wondering if Adele would be able to manage here by herself. Without her makeup and fine clothes, she looked younger, and even though her face registered discomfort, she looked oddly beautiful. The stony façade that kept people at a distance was gone, along with the piercing look that caused others to look away or shift their weight from one foot to another. But also gone was the look of being impervious to outside forces.

Adele Harrington looked vulnerable.

"Po," Adele started, looking up from her chair. "Po, do you think—"

Po waited, but the sentence hung there in the air for so long, Po wondered if Adele had forgotten what she was going to ask. "Yes?" she prompted.

"Do you think it's time I threw in the towel?"

It wasn't what Po expected. And for a minute, she wasn't completely sure what Adele was asking. But as she watched her swivel her head and look around the room, the big, beautiful old home, she knew exactly what Adele was suggesting.

"And move away, you mean? Sell the home, pack up your dream?"

Adele nodded slowly. "I'm a strong woman. I've had to be independent for a long time. My mother urged me out of this house and into a world in which women had the disadvantage. But I've always held my own. Always. I'm not sure I've ever really been happy. But I succeeded in everything I tried."

Po sat down and listened as Adele went on. "This house was never mine, you know. Coming back after Ollie died, I thought maybe I could make it mine. Fill it with people. Pull up the memories I have that are good, bury the others. I thought I could bring back my mother and my brother somehow, adding beauty to this place they loved."

"You can, Adele. It's going to be a magnificent place."

"But what is happening around me? Someone doesn't want me here. That's clear. Someone wants this house in a terrible, insane way. And how many people will be hurt while I stubbornly hang on to it?" Adele winced as she tried to shift in the chair.

"You can't let others rule your life." Po walked over to the sink and refilled Adele's water glass. She looked out at the workman pulling ladders and toolboxes from their trucks. A gardener pushed a wheelbarrow out to the backyard, and in the distance, she heard someone whistling a light cheerful tune. She turned from the sink and felt an enormous resolve.

"Adele," Po said. "You can't let anyone take this away from you. This is your home. Somehow, I promise you, we will bring an end to the bad things happening here. And you will be at home again. Now let's get on with it."

Chapter 20

Despite the fact that gossip sometimes ran rampant in Crestwood, when push came to shove, it was a place where neighbors looked out for neighbors. And when Po made a call to Leah's husband, Tim, and asked him to stop by on his way home from his busy pediatric practice to check the sprained ankle of a fifty-two-year-old woman, she knew the favor would be granted.

"She'll be fine, Po," Tim assured her when he called later that evening. "Adele has a couple of crutches to help her around for the next few days, but she's one determined lady, and I don't think anything as minor as a fat ankle will keep her down for long."

Po smiled into the phone at the description of Adele. She was a strong lady, for sure. But she also had a soft spot. And Po suspected that it would widen in time.

"By the way," Tim added. "Leah mentioned to me that Adele had boarded her dog the day of the fire and it was raising some eyebrows. Sounded suspicious, I suppose."

"Yes?" Po hadn't addressed that with Adele. But she knew—she hoped—there was a reason, because Tim was correct—it was very suspicious.

"Well, she mentioned to me that she had had the yard sprayed," Tim said. "She wondered if I thought she was being overly protective by not wanting Emerson around the chemicals. I told her no, that I thought she was one wise lady who cared a lot about her dog. I'd have done the same. Those chemicals are awful for dogs. And kids," Tim added, before hanging up the phone.

For a brief moment, Po felt a wash of shame for doubting Adele's motives. And then great relief, and then she sighed in a satisfied way and continued with her phone calls.

A call to Eleanor assured Po that Adele would have food the next day. Eleanor would stop by with groceries, a stack of her travel magazines, and a deck of cards. And Kate said she'd check in on Adele periodically as she biked by the house.

And Po herself would help out by donning an old pair of jeans and a Canterbury sweatshirt, and begin rummaging through the charred remains of Joe's apartment, saving Adele the grief of doing so herself.

"Thank you, Po," Adele said when Po showed up the next Thursday morning. "I don't know why you are all pitching in like this. But I—"

"Oh, shush," Po said. "It's what we do."

"Well, you do it well," Adele allowed. She sat in a sunroom just off the kitchen, her foot wrapped in a flesh-colored bandage and elevated on a small stool. Windows surrounded her on three sides, and she could easily monitor the activity and comings and goings of the workman without moving an inch. To the side, spread out on a low coffee table, were piles of papers, forms, and a laptop computer.

"This looks like command central, Adele." The color had come back into Adele's high cheekbones, and she was dressed comfortably today in loose slacks and a silky teal blouse. She looked quite beautiful, Po thought.

Adele nodded. "They don't know it, but with that window open," Adele nodded to a window next to the couch, "I can hear everything they say. It's an education, believe me."

"I've no doubt." Po laughed.

"But the sad thing is," Adele continued, watching the men beyond her window, "some of them are refusing to come to work. The crew has diminished considerably in the past week."

Po frowned. "I didn't realize that."

"They don't want to be connected to what's happening here. They hate it that television cameras stop by and film them. But the real reason, I know, is that they hear the rumors, too. They know that some people think I killed Joe—and some who think I killed my brother. I can't say I blame the workmen for not wanting to be here. But I can't afford to be without them. Every delay costs me money."

There was genuine sadness shadowing Adele's face, and Po had a powerful urge to find the contractor and give him a piece of her mind. Whatever happened to innocent until proven guilty. "Would you like some coffee before I tackle the carriage house?"

Adele shook her head no. "I don't know how bad it is up there, Po, but it should be safe. The fireman said they were able to control it before the foundation was weakened." She looked across the drive at the open windows and charred sills of the garage apartment. "If it's too awful and the smell is too bad, please don't stay. I don't think there's much of value up there. My mother filled the place with old cast-off books from our library, hoping Joe Bates might educate himself. He never seemed very interested though. All I really care about are things of Oliver's—please save them for me. Contrary to that librarian's rantings, I would never have thrown anything of my brother's away."

"I think Halley is still emotional over Oliver's death, Adele. I don't think she means those things."

"Oh, Po, that's where you're wrong. She means them. But for the life of me, I don't know where her accusations are coming from."

Po picked up her work gloves and a couple of cardboard boxes she had brought with her. She didn't want to argue with Adele. Besides, she had a point. Halley did seem to attack Adele rather severely. She wondered about that, and also what the young woman thought she could possibly find in Joe's apartment that was worth trespassing and angering Adele. Maybe once she spent a little time up there herself she'd have a better understanding of Halley's obsession with it.

"Well, I'm off," she said to Adele. "You can call me on my cell if you need anything. I've left the number there beside your computer."

Adele waved her hand in the air. "I'm fine. I get around quite nicely on these crutches—and they make nice battering poles should anyone give me trouble."

Po took several plastic bags from the kitchen and hurried across the drive and up the back steps of the carriage house. It was a bright, crisp fall day, and the clean air was a sharp contrast to the awful stench on the other side of Joe Bates's door. Po walked in cautiously, feeling the presence of the old man who had kept to himself so severely these past years.

Light from the open windows and a skylight above revealed a soot-filled, damp room with a small galley kitchen at one end. Off to one side, Po walked into a room with a bed and dresser, cluttered now with burnt ceiling tiles scattered everywhere.

Remnants of barely recognizable personal items—a hairbrush and floppy hat, books, and a reading lamp—lay like lumps of coal on the floor. Here and there small puddles of water remained, reminders of the firemen's attack against the flames. And everywhere was the pungent odor of burnt matter.

Joe's place must have been cozy before the fire created such havoc, Po thought, walking back into the living room and looking around. Built-in blackened bookcases filled an interior wall, and a small brass telescope lay on its side on a table near a window. A gift from Oliver, Po suspected. Some things escaped the flames, Po noticed, but almost nothing escaped the force of the water that put them out. An old, overstuffed chair and couch, pushed now to the center of the room, was wet and lumpy, burned on one side but not the other. Po sighed. The remains of a long life reduced to rubble.

The sadness that came over her was unexpected—and profound.

To work, she told herself. There will be time for dealing with sad thoughts later.

After slipping on her work gloves, Po walked carefully to the bookcase, stepping over broken dishes and burnt dishtowels, black flakes of newspapers and chunks of canned food that had exploded from the heat.

Some of the shelves held nothing but charred clumps of the Harringtons' old books that Adele had mentioned. But on other shelves, the books were still recognizable. She carefully pulled one from the shelf and read the darkened spine. It was Rudyard Kipling's *Jungle Book*, and she tried to think of old Joe, sitting in his chair by the window, reading it. Perhaps Adele was wrong and Joe Bates read avidly, devouring these classics. One never knew everything about another's life. The thought of Joe steeping himself in reading pleased Po. You could learn much about a person from the books they read. She set the book on the floor near her stash of garbage sacks, thinking it might be salvageable—and perhaps even a collector's item.

For an hour Po rummaged through books and charred papers, scattered across the shelves and on the floor. She collected those that were still intact and made a small pile near the door, then added some framed pictures of Oliver and his mother that were wavy beneath the glass but still intact. There was a picture of Oliver and Joe, and one of a young Oliver—perhaps twenty or so—standing next to a beautiful young woman. Po took it over to the window and looked at it more closely in the sunlight, rubbing the surface clean with her finger. Only in the bright natural light did Po realize the woman was Adele. She was standing next to her brother, smiling into the camera. Po took a piece of paper towel and rubbed the cracked glass. Adele and Ollie. Happy. Po wrapped the picture in folds of paper towel to protect it and added it to her pile.

A solid old rolltop desk, its legs darkened by the fire but still holding up the top, stood a few feet from the bookshelf. It was a massive thing, Po saw, and seemed to have resisted the fire by its very boldness. The curved rolltop, swollen with water and singed by flames, stuck when Po tried to slide it up, but a few strong tugs and it gave way. Inside, Po found more of Joe's life—pads of paper, damp bills, pens and pencils, and several small books, as well as some legal-looking documents that were waterlogged and curled.

Po pressed one flat and could read Ollie's name at the bottom, but the rest was smeared and indecipherable. She frowned. Odd. And somewhat unsettling. Po thought about all the claims on Oliver's house, and the thought that he might have written up a will before he died surfaced briefly, then disappeared beneath the weight of the task in front of her. Po gathered what papers were intact and set them beside the door to look at later.

The cubbyholes in the old desk were stuffed with bank books and scraps of papers, a small garden guide filled with newspaper clippings on gardening and notes Joe must have written to himself. She picked up a still-intact book jacket, soggy now and darkened from heat. *A Plain Man's Guide to a Starry Night.* She smiled at the thought of Joe reading the book, maybe sitting by the window, looking up at the night sky that Jed had written about in his book. Yes, Adele was wrong. Joe *did* read. And he read books that Ollie would have liked, perhaps that Ollie had encouraged his friend to read.

Po piled the desk contents into a box and continued poking through the cavernous lower cabinet of the old desk, pulling out more pictures, an old pipe that still had tobacco packed tightly inside the bowl, and a whole stack of legal-sized yellow pads of paper. Po smiled at the pads. She and Joe had something in common—capturing thoughts on yellow pads of paper. Po had them lying all over her house. She picked one up and realized it was Ollie's, his familiar, neat printing filling the lines. Notes from a class, it looked like, and another cited books from the library, and in the margin of one, she spotted Halley's name and a small heart doodled next to it. *This is the kind of thing Halley must have been looking for,* she thought. The things she had shared with Ollie and that Joe had taken from his room before Adele arrived. Po scooped up the pads and added them to her stash. Perhaps she would give Halley the pad with her name on it—a small reminder of how much Ollie cared about her. It would mean something to Halley, and Adele surely wouldn't want it.

A few hours later, Po decided she had done all she could do and the rest could be done by workmen who would remove the debris and prepare the small apartment for its renovation. She hailed a painter walking behind the house and had him help her pile the salvageable things in boxes—the telescope and a couple of lamps that had escaped the fire's wrath. Some silverware that might have belonged to Adele's mother. Po decided Adele should see them and decide their fate. She directed the painter to carry some of the boxes over to the house, storing them for now in the basement where the smell wouldn't bother Adele.

The other things—the desk contents, some books, a pile of photographs, and the yellow pads—she piled in boxes and carried to her car. She'd dry them out at home and return to Adele anything that might have memories of Ollie attached to it.

A day's work well done, she thought, driving down the driveway and tugging her cell phone from the pocket of her jeans. She was pleased that she had relieved Adele of a task that would clearly be a burden to her.

And now that Adele was settled and she'd removed personal things from the carriage house, there were other things Po needed to put her mind to. Phoebe, bless her platinum head, was right this time. Things were moving too slowly, and a woman's reputation was at stake—and maybe her life. Something had to be done soon to salvage Adele Harrington's reputation—and what could soon be a beautiful bed and breakfast inn at 210 Kingfish Drive.

Po paused at the end of the drive and pushed the buttons on her small silver phone. "P.J.," she said out loud. "How wonderful that I've caught you. How would you like to share a bowl of spicy shrimp soup with me tonight?"

Chapter 21

"I'm only here because of your cooking, Po," P.J. said, standing over the stove and stirring the rich coconut milk broth. He closed his eyes and breathed in the pungent smell of garlic, ginger, and parsley. "It's definitely not the fact that I strongly suspect I'm being lured here for other, less delicious motives."

Po smiled and put two placemats out on the oak table that had been the heart of the Paltrow home for thirty years. Small indentations along the surface spoke of years of homework, games being played, and friends gathering to argue politics, literature, and philosophies of life while eating and drinking in the warmth of the Paltrow family room.

"Better set three, Po," P.J. said, glancing at the table.

"Kate knows you're here?"

P.J. nodded. He scooped up a small amount of soup in a ladle and tasted it. "This is fantastic. You've outdone yourself, Po." He walked across the kitchen to the small bar in the family room bookcase and began mixing gin and ice cubes in a silver shaker. "Kate doesn't care about me, Po," he said over his shoulder. "I made the mistake of mentioning your Thai soup."

Po pulled out another placemat. She had purposely not called Kate because she didn't want her around when she talked to P.J. about the murders. But that was probably silly. Kate had never fit nicely in a cocoon, and Po's instinct to put her there whenever there was a chance of anything bordering on danger or sadness was irrational, if heartfelt. And as usual she'd made enough soup for an army, planning on taking some over to Adele the next day and freezing the rest.

"Kate had a yearbook meeting with the high school kids but will be here when it's over. She was skipping pizza for your Thai soup."

"I'm honored," Po said. The sound of a car in the driveway announced Kate's arrival, but when Po looked over at the back door, it was Leah coming in, a deep rust corduroy skirt swishing around her ankles and a hand-woven scarf wrapped around her neck. And just a step behind her was Jed Fellers.

"It's getting chilly out there," Leah said, taking off a short wool jacket and hanging it on a hook by the door. "I hope you don't mind my barging in, Po. Jed and I had a committee meeting, and I convinced him that the only antidote for it was a bowl of that soup you told me you were making tonight. Tim was on call, and I needed to be with people." She waved across the room at P.J. and gave Po a hug. "And I convinced Jed that he did, too."

Behind her, Jed smiled sheepishly. "Hope it's okay, Po. Leah makes it difficult to say no."

"Of course I don't mind," Po said, smelling the bouquet of flowers Jed handed her. "I'd have been offended if you had said no, Jed."

"It's all this unrest," Leah went on, searching in Po's cupboard for a vase. "I feel it on campus every day. Bad vibes everywhere."

"The students are confused," Jed agreed. "It's a tense time." He took the vase from Leah and filled it with water.

Po pulled out a couple more placemats. "The soup will ease the chill. But you're absolutely right about the tension. The neighborhood is filled with bad energy. And, unfortunately, it's going to take more than soup to get rid of it. How is Halley handling it all, Jed?"

Jed thought for a minute before answering. He put the flowers in the vase, set it aside, and leaned back against the counter. "I think she's doing all right. We're both wondering now if we'll ever know who is at the bottom of all this. Halley is trying to accept that, trying to move on."

"I was inclined to think that myself. But the fire changed that. It brought the presence of someone evil closer to us again, not someone who did those awful deeds, then skipped town."

"There's the possibility that they're not connected," Leah said.

Po thought about that and looked over at P.J. He was being unusually quiet. He had suggested the same thing—that perhaps there wasn't a link.

But Po didn't buy it. There were connections between all the happenings at the B&B, she felt sure of it. Unfortunately, feelings didn't solve crimes. She needed some facts.

A minute later, Kate breezed through the back door. She strode across the kitchen and dropped her shopping bag on the counter. "French bread from Jacques's, pricey wine and a hunk of cheese from Brew and Brie. Oh, and Marla's cheesecake. Elderberry Road in a bag. I figured since I wasn't really invited I'd sweeten my presence." She planted a kiss on Po's cheek and hugged Leah.

"Come here, woman," P.J. bellowed in a deep feigned accent from the other end of the room. "What am I—chopped liver?" He put down the martini shaker and spread his arms wide.

Kate walked across the room and into his embrace, wrapping her arms around his waist. Her hair brushed his cheek. "Hi, you," she said into his chest.

P.J. breathed in her scent. "Katie, you smell almost as good as Po's soup."

"And you smell like gin." Kate pulled her head back and looked into P.J.'s wide smile. A lock of sandy hair fell across his forehead, and she brushed it back with her finger, then pulled away. "Enough PDA. I'll leave you to your shaking, Flanigan. Make mine with an olive, please." Kate moved back to the cupboards and began pulling out platters for the cheese and bread.

Po walked over to the floor-to-ceiling stone fireplace that filled one end of the open living area. She pulled back the mesh screen. "I know it's early in the season, but somehow a fire seems in order tonight."

"My job," Jed said. "I'll put my Eagle Scout training to work."

"Good idea," Leah said, and carried the cheese and crackers platter to the coffee table. "Maybe it will warm our bones a bit." She slipped out of her clunky clogs and settled down on the overstuffed couch, feet tucked up beneath her.

Po sat beside her and accepted a glass from P.J. "Maybe we'll even warm each other's spirit." She sipped the martini slowly, enjoying the tingly sensation as it ran down her throat. The evening hadn't turned out exactly as she had planned—a private talk with P.J. to pull what information she could out of him about the investigation into Ollie's and Joe's deaths. Although he wasn't working the case, he always knew what was going on, especially when it was as personal and close to home as this case was. She wanted an update, wanted him to know she was absolutely convinced that Adele had no part in any of the bad things that were happening in their neighborhood.

She wanted him to help salvage what was left of a proud woman's reputation. Maybe even her life.

Kate stepped into her thoughts. "I stopped by on my way over here to check on Adele." She had curled up on the opposite couch, her long, jeans-clad legs twisted like a pretzel beneath her. A red cashmere sweater that Po had given her for Christmas last year matched the blush the fire was bringing to her cheeks. "She's one gutsy woman. Tom Adler stopped by while I was there. That guy just doesn't give up. He left his wife out in his Beemer and barged right into the house. He suggested the time had come for Adele to sell the place before she ruined the whole town. His words, certainly not mine." Kate cut a piece of cheese and handed it to Leah.

"What?" Po sat up straight, nearly spilling her martini down the front of her black turtleneck. "What is he talking about?"

"He insinuated that Adele was personally responsible for two murders, a fire, nervous neighbors, and the loss of business to the town because people were afraid to come to Crestwood with her around."

"The man is certifiably crazy," Leah said.

"And desperate," P.J. said.

Jed stoked the fire until the embers were glowing and flames began lapping at the bricks, then sat nearby where he could give it a poke when needed. "Adler came into Jacques's the other night. He'd been drinking pretty heavily and Jacques asked him to leave. I think the fellow has some personal problems."

"He's in some financial trouble, but that's no excuse for that kind of behavior. Adele should have accused him of trespassing," Po said.

"Oh, she did," Kate said. "She threatened to call the police, and I think she would have, but the damsel waiting for Tom became impatient and began honking the horn. Tom went running."

"He's such an angry man," Leah said. "I wonder if he had anything to do with this."

"He certainly has motive," Kate said. "He's been acting crazy ever since marrying again. I think this new wife has high expectations for him—especially when it comes to money."

"That would be enough to make someone desperate, I suppose," Po said. But she wasn't completely convinced. There was something about Tom Adler that was far more show than substance. But if not he, then who could have murdered the two men who lived at 210 Kingfish Drive—one so gentle and naïve, and the other an old gardener whose sole goal was to protect Ollie Harrington from harm and keep his pond free of algae?

"How about we have some soup?" P.J. announced. "It smells ready and I'm starving."

"P.J., if I ever open a restaurant, will you be my sandwich board guy?" Po asked.

"Your what?" P.J. asked, wrinkling his forehead. "Po, I'm far too young to know about sandwich boards." He waved the others over. "Come on folks, get it while it's hot. Jed, want to open a bottle of wine?"

Jed helped himself to a corkscrew and poured glasses all around while chairs were pulled back and soup poured into bowls with rice lining the bottoms.

"Where's Max?" Kate asked, leaning in to light the candles.

"He was going to stop by Adele's too. The renovation is taking longer than it should, and Max was going to help her check her financial situation." Po repeated the news about the workers slowing down and staying away, not wanting to be connected with a murder scene.

"That's awful," Kate said. "This whole thing is awful. Phoebe's right— we should all don black jeans and turtlenecks and snoop around until we solve this thing. I've been thinking we are all going down the wrong path. What if it doesn't have anything to do with someone wanting to own the Harrington property?"

"What else makes sense?" Jed asked.

"I don't know," Kate replied. "But if teaching high school kids has taught me anything, it's that things are rarely what they seem to be."

Po had been thinking the same thing. So, what *was* going on here? What were they missing? Was it Adele herself? Was she back in Crestwood for reasons no one knew? Was there a family thing going on, something between the Harringtons and another family in town? The Adlers, maybe? Or maybe Ollie and Joe were mixed up in, something that had gotten them in trouble. Drugs? There were always rumors of people selling to the college kids. The thought was so ludicrous and uncomfortable that it made Po grimace.

"Are you all right?" P.J. asked.

"Yes," Po answered, brushing off his concern. She forced a smile to her face. "I was just trying to sort through some things. Seconds, anyone?"

* * * *

When Max stopped by a while later, Po's impromptu dinner companions had moved into the night—P.J. and Kate to walk along the river path while the weather still afforded it, Leah home to deliver a leftover container of soup to a tired husband. And Jed was headed to the campus library to walk Halley home from her late-night shift. And she hadn't had a single moment to dump her concerns on P.J., other than the general talk that filtered in and out of the dinner conversation.

Po sat alone in the darkened family room, the lights dim and the dying embers of the fire casting shadows on the pine-planked floor. In the distance Segovia's magic fingers strummed flamenco music. "Hi, Max," she said, watching her friend walk across the kitchen. "Please don't mind if I stay put. I'm exhausted. There's leftover soup in the fridge."

Max strode across the room and kissed Po on the forehead, then busied himself at the small bar. He mixed a Scotch and soda and finally sat down beside her. A sigh followed a long swallow of his drink.

"Good sigh or bad?"

"Long day. Adele's not a bad lady, Po."

Po moved her head in agreement.

"But what's happening around her is not good. The workers are making things difficult. And rumors are spreading around the neighborhood that there's a murderer in their midst, maybe next door, down the street."

"Who's spreading those rumors?"

Max shrugged. "Some well-intentioned folks, probably—there are some elderly people who live on that street and they're understandably concerned. For a quiet neighborhood, there's a lot of unusual activity at 210 Kingfish Drive. And then there are others—people like the moms in Phoebe's playgroup. And some with other motives, like Tom Adler and College Board members who would love to get their hands on the property." Max looped an arm around the back of the couch and took another drink.

"It's not a good situation for Adele, that's for sure. Bed and breakfasts conjure up images of cozy bedrooms and warm scones for breakfast, not arson and dead bodies floating in ponds." Po looked into the crackling flames, watching flecks of gold shoot up the chimney. "Kate said something tonight that got me thinking. Something about things not being what they seem to be."

"Sure. Let's hope. If they are what they seem to be, Adele is suspect number one and Adler and Halley are probably tied for second place."

"Halley?"

"I know. Doesn't seem likely. Especially when it comes to Ollie. But the fire? She was there..."

"And so was Adele. But what if the motive isn't the property at all. What if it's something else?"

Max listened and nodded. "Could be something right in front of our noses. And all we need to do is step back a bit to see it."

But they both knew that stepping back could also be dangerous.

* * * *

In her dreams that night, Po stepped back as far as she could, and as darkness folded in around her, she felt herself falling off a cliff. Suddenly, in the blackness, the fall was stopped and she was caught in strong, familiar arms. She awoke with a start, sitting up in bed, her heart beating wildly. As the fog and fear cleared from her head and her heart slowed, Po looked up at the moonlight streaming in the window. Scott's presence was so real that Po thought for a minute she could reach out and touch the arms that rescued her.

"So, my darling," she said aloud, "what would you have me do now?" But she knew the answer, even without Scott wrapping strong arms around her, holding her close.

My darling Po, tread lightly and safely, he'd say.

And then he'd pull those thick brows together and try to look at her sternly, but the look would be more one of loving concern, tinged with great pride as he whispered to be careful.

But the time was right—time to get all their lives out of limbo. Time to start living again.

Chapter 22

Po briefly drifted off, but was up with the first light. She plugged in the coffee pot and filled Hoover's bowl with fresh water. It was too early to approach the world beyond her doors, so she'd begin instead with what was close by, anything that would bring her closer to understanding the lives of the two men who had lived on the lavish Harrington estate. And perhaps in understanding their lives and their friendship, she'd come closer to understanding why they had died.

There was plenty of Joe and Ollie's lives spread out in her basement, drying in the warm furnace-heated air. She had laid them out, then left them alone without another glance. A good place to start.

Po poured herself a mug of coffee, flicked the light switch in the back kitchen hallway, and headed down the narrow stairs. The pungent odor of the remains of a fire assaulted her. She stopped on the steps for a moment, adjusting to it, then continued on down.

Scott and Po had finished one side of their basement as a playroom for the kids years ago, just after Sophie was born. The knotty-pine walls spoke of another era but held warm memories, as did the eight-foot table that had hosted countless birthday parties, Cub Scout projects, and craft sessions—and sometimes doubled for a noisy game of Ping-Pong. Today it was spread end-to-end with remnants of Joe Bates's carriage house apartment—pads of paper, books propped open to encourage drying, photographs, and small paintings of flowers that she suspected Joe had done himself. When she'd emptied the boxes, Po had discovered that she'd brought home more than she had intended. And there was still a box that she'd forgotten in her car.

But more was better, and she'd get around to it all. Spread it all out, dry it, and return to Adele what was salvageable. The pictures, especially. Adele would want those. She set to work, carefully removing the photos from their frames, pressing them smooth, and placing them on paper towels.

Carefully, she peeled away small pieces of paper stuck inside books, some written on in Ollie's careful handwriting. The distinctive blend of printing and cursive was intriguing and unmistakable.

She smoothed out the pages torn from a yellow legal pad, wondering absently what people would find out about her if someday they went through her books, her papers, her small notebooks filled with thoughts and ideas and lines from poetry she loved. Would they be able to interpret the underlinings, the notes in the margin, the dozens of small pieces of paper and sticky notes she'd put in a book to save her place, or on which she'd copied a line she especially liked? Ollie had made plenty of notes on scraps of paper, perhaps intended to teach Joe, to help him understand the stars, the heavens, the things that Ollie loved.

She picked up the copy of Jed's book. She'd have to buy a copy of it one of these days. Gus had sold out, but was going to order more for the store. There were notes in the column here, too. Some washed away by the firemen's efforts, but others still intact, with passages underlined and handwritten stars scribbled next to favorite passages.

The ringing of her phone startled Po for a minute, then drew her out of her thoughts and up the basement stairs where she'd left it on the counter.

"Hi, Po. Are you up?"

"Have I ever slept beyond seven o'clock in my entire life?" Po set her empty coffee cup in the sink and looked out into the deep green of her backyard. The oak leaves were beginning to turn, and there was already a light coating of maple leaves on the ground, scattered now as Hoover chased a squirrel around a bed of mums.

"Sorry, Po," Kate said. "It seemed a logical question when you're calling someone at eight in the morning."

"Why aren't you at school?"

"There's a teachers' conference in Kansas City. It seemed optional, so I stayed behind. I need to run by the college to pick up some books, but after that, you up for coffee? Your place?"

"Better yet, let's meet at the college. The new coffee house is carrying Peet's coffee. Give me an hour."

Po closed the basement door and headed upstairs. She took a quick shower and slipped into a pair of light corduroy slacks and a soft gray turtleneck. Heeding the weatherman's advice, she grabbed a jacket, called Hoover inside, then headed out.

She had planned to pick up some books at the college library today—and hopefully, to run into Halley Peterson.

Po walked the few blocks to the college—she would never get used to calling it Canterbury *University*—a bit pretentious, she thought. Stuffy. The opposite of the campus that had been a second home to her for so many years.

She hurried across the quad, stepping aside several times for students burdened with massive backpacks passing her by. One wall of the coffee shop was nearly all glass, and through it she spotted Kate, commandeering two leather chairs and a small round table. Po hurried in.

"Got here just in time," Kate said. "The place is a zoo with everyone wanting their start-the-day jolt of java."

Po dropped her bag beside the chair and sat down. She looked around, taking stock of the crowded, early morning crowd. Halley Peterson waved at her from her place in line across the room, and Po waved back, motioning for her to join them when she was through. "She's one of the reasons I wanted to stop by the college today," Po said, nodding toward the librarian. "You don't mind, do you, Kate?"

"Nope, not at all. I like Halley—and she someone we should be talking to even if I didn't like her. P.J. and I ran into her the other night at Jacques's. She and Jed Fellers came in for dinner. In spite of everything, they seemed to be having a good time. At least that's how it looked—lots of gabbing going on and Halley had a pretty blush to her cheeks. I think difficult times can bring people together more quickly than the normal course of living."

"She does seem a little happier, though I know Ollie's and Joe's deaths have taken a toll on her. I'm glad she has Jed to help her through it."

"Sometimes we forget that Jed is going through all this, too. Leah said he and Ollie were close."

Halley walked over to their table with coffee and a cinnamon roll. "You don't mind?" she asked, putting down her mug and pulling over an empty chair from the wall. She was smiling.

"A new haircut?" Po asked. She looked more closely and realized it was the first time she'd seen Halley with makeup, and her usual jeans had given way to a skirt and soft cashmere sweater. "You look lovely," Po said.

Halley blushed. "I've decided that shabby wasn't chic on me."

"You were never shabby, but you do look great," Kate said.

"So what's new? Is there any news?" Halley asked, clearly anxious to divert attention from herself.

"Well, you may have heard that Adele Harrington sprained her ankle," Po began.

Halley frowned. "I didn't know that."

"She was going up to clean out Joe's place after that awful fire," Kate explained. "Po found her."

"Did she do it?"

"Do what?" Po asked.

"Clean out the apartment?" Halley said.

Po was quiet for a moment, wondering why Halley seemed to skip over the more obvious question about Adele's injury.

Halley seemed to read Po's thoughts and said quickly, "I don't mean to seem uncaring about Adele Harrington. She and I simply don't see eye to eye on things. I think it might just be that we handle our emotions, our grief, differently. But I hope she's okay. I certainly don't wish her ill."

"I understand. Adele hasn't been very understanding about your friendship with her brother."

Halley ran her fingers through her hair and shook her head. When she spoke, her voice had an edge to it that seemed out of place, coming from the quiet librarian. "No, she hasn't. And I don't know…I still think Adele maybe knows more about Ollie's death than she's saying. I'm not sure Ollie wanted Adele to have the house."

"Who should have it? Adele grew up there, too," Kate said.

Halley stared at her plate. Finally, she looked up. "I don't know. Maybe… maybe me. I told him that was silly, but I don't think he had many people he was close to. And he wanted the house cared for."

"Ollie told you he had changed his will?" Po asked.

"Well, sort of."

"And that's why you think Adele had something to do with his death? That seems severe, Halley. Ollie was her twin brother and her only sibling. I don't know how you can make that leap."

Halley nodded. "At first I couldn't imagine someone killing her own brother. But it happens all the time. Most murders are within families." She looked at Po, then Kate. "It's true," she said.

Po listened intently, watching belief fill Halley's eyes. Her words seemed to strengthen her resolve and the smile fell from her face as she talked.

"Well, it's not true in this case," Kate said.

"But you don't know that," Halley said. "There are things you don't know about Adele Harrington. She's greedy, she's not a good person."

"Why do you think that, Halley?" Po asked. "I know Adele is abrupt and can even be rude, but she has had an enormous amount of grief to bear these weeks. Her life has been pulled apart. Your judgment seems unduly harsh."

Halley bit down on her bottom lip, as if preventing herself from saying something she might regret. She looked at Po, her eyes flashing. "I believe what I believe. And I respect that you have your own convictions. You're wrong, though." She pushed back her chair and forced a smile to her face. "I better get over to the library. My shift starts in a few minutes."

Po and Kate watched as Halley dropped her napkin and paper plate into the refuse container, then took her cup and hurried out the door. They watched through the glass as she stopped and waved at someone.

Jed Fellers was walking across the quad, an armload of books in his hand and a student at his side. He returned her wave along with a broad smile. As if by magic, the concern and consternation fell from Halley's face. In its place was a bright look of joy.

"Now I understand the change in dress. The makeup," Kate said.

"Halley Peterson is in love," Po finished.

"I wonder if she's shared her dislike of Adele Harrington with Jed?"

"Probably not. Jed has been supportive of Adele. I don't think Adele trusts people easily, and Jed hasn't quite received a warm welcome, but he's been gentlemanly about trying to help where he can."

"Why do you think Halley is so concerned about Joe's apartment?" Kate asked.

"I think she just wants some remembrance of Ollie. Maybe it's just a sentimental thing."

Kate shook her head. "It doesn't ring true to me, Po. Her efforts to retrieve something of Ollie's seem kind of weird. She has her memories, and surely Joe would have given her what he thought Ollie might want her to have."

"Actually, I agree with you. I wanted to ask her about it, but it didn't seem like the right time."

Kate nibbled on her scone. "So what do you think? Why has Halley continued to barge into Adele's life when she's been told to stay away?"

Po drained her cup. Why indeed. What was Halley Peterson thinking?

Po and Kate went their separate ways with promises to talk later.

But between now and then, Kate explained that she was heading to the park to take some photos. And to think about Ollie Harrington and Joe Bates. And Tom Adler, and Adele and Halley. She confessed to Po that she'd had dreams about them all the night before. She was walking through a forest, following Joe and Ollie. And they kept nearing the edge of the woods where the trees fell away and sunlight flooded the rutted ground.

But they never quite reached the light. They were always a few footsteps away. And the darkness kept getting deeper.

A few footsteps away. Po thought. She felt that, too. The pieces were scattered all around them. If only they could scoop them up and fit them into the right places, perhaps they could bring some closure—bring some light into the darkness—before someone else got hurt.

That thought was never far from Po's mind. She went home and put in a load of wash, trying to shake the awful foreboding that weighed heavy on her. She ran Hoover over to Maggie's for a checkup, then finally settled down in her den to work on an article she was writing for a quilting magazine. She'd been asked to write about the origin of quilting bees, and describe how their own local quilting group worked, sewing together art and friendship. A topic close to her heart. It would practically write itself.

But after an hour of staring at an empty screen, Po realized her mind was too full of other things. It was futile to sit there any longer. Instead, she reached for a yellow pad and began to doodle. Somehow, writing down scattered thoughts sometimes made them more comprehensible. She and Ollie, perhaps, were alike in that way.

Ollie. Joe.

People on her mind. Two good friends.

House. Apartment.

It occurred to Po that dwellings figured prominently in the lives of these friends. Bound them together. She scribbled on the pad, drew circles around their names. Doodled stick figures. And stars.

Halley.

Halley seemed to love the Harrington house almost as much as Ollie had. Perhaps that was why she loved it—because it had been his. And Halley thought Ollie had wanted her to have it. An odd thought for casual friends. If the words carried truth, Ollie seemed to have promised his house to many people. Maybe it was Ollie's way to avoid conflict. To win friends.

Po frowned. She looked again at her pad. Ollie's name. Joe's. And Halley's. Halley had wanted something from Joe's apartment. But there was little there. Writings of Ollie's? But why? Sentimental reasons maybe. Something more? Something about the house. Revised wills? Notes of intent? Did Halley know something about Ollie that might help find his murderer? As much as she didn't want to distrust Halley, she agreed with Kate that there was something odd about it all.

Po hadn't had the chance she was looking for to talk with Halley. Maybe tomorrow she'd invite her to come look through the things from

Joe's apartment. There was a picture she knew she would like. Halley and Ollie out beside the pond. Po wondered if Joe had taken it.

Such an odd, unlikely threesome.

Po began squinting at her own words and realized while she'd doodled, the room had grown dark. She looked over at the clock above her stove and pushed back her chair. Max would be there soon to pick her up. They were taking Eleanor to Jacques's for her birthday. A most welcome treat to take their minds off fires and suspicions and people's pain.

But first she'd call Halley. She pulled a card Halley had given her earlier from her purse and tapped in the numbers on her cell, suspecting Halley might still be at work and not checking her cell. She left a brief message, that she had found something at Joe's that Halley might like. Then she hurried upstairs to dress.

The message would bring Halley over, she thought. And then they could talk. Po suspected Halley had answers that Po didn't even know the questions to.

Chapter 23

Po, Max, and Eleanor arrived at Jacques's early, hoping to beat the usual Friday night crowd. "The better to hear you, my dears," Eleanor said, confessing that the din in restaurants was beginning to bother her eighty-three-year-old ears.

Max laughed. "El, you're amazing. I've been bothered by loud noises for years. What's your secret?"

"Jacques's escargots. One plate a day keeps everything working just fine." She smiled up into the round face of the restaurant owner. "And how are you, dear Jacques?"

He leaned down and kissed Eleanor on each cheek, then repeated his European ritual with Po. "Beautiful ladies, you honor me tonight with your presence."

"Oh, shush, Jacques," Po said, waving her hand in the air. "You say that to all the women."

"But never with such passion, dear Po," Jacques said, his clear blue eyes twinkling. "That I reserve only for you, *mon amie*."

"It looks like we're not the only ones coming in early," Max observed, looking around.

Jacques nodded. "Business is good tonight, but not so good other nights. Bad vibrations from the Harrington house are invading our Elderberry shops." He waved one plump hand in the air. "Go away, bad vibrations."

"I know, Jacques. It's a bad thing."

"But maybe it is solved tonight."

"Oh? What do you mean, Jacques?" Po pushed her glasses up into her hair.

"Monsignor Adler—he was around here earlier—out on the sidewalk. Drunk as a skunk, as you say here in America. Shouting awful things at Madame Harrington."

"Adele? She was here?"

"Yes, she was here in my restaurant, her ankle bandaged and swollen, but her face quite beautiful. She came in for dinner on the arm of Professor Fellers. A magnificent-looking couple, those two."

"Jed Fellers and Adele?" Po's brows lifted.

Max frowned. "That's odd. Jed told me Adele doesn't give him the time of day, and I've seen her be rude to him."

"Maybe she changed her mind," Eleanor said. "People do that, you know."

"Agreed. I think it's good that she's getting out," Po said. "Was Halley Peterson with them, too? A younger woman, brown hair—"

Jacques shook his head. "Non. Just the two of them. They had drinks, then my escargots. The professor was gentlemanly and gracious, but he was a little uncomfortable, I think. Not quite himself. And then that awful man began banging on the window, threatening Madame Harrington. The professor shielded her, moved her away from the window."

"What happened then?" Po asked.

"I hurried outside to stop him from making such a scene in front of my bistro, but the police were already there, and they took him away. He was frightening my customers. And Madame Harrington was clearly upset at the public display."

"And then?" Eleanor asked, nudging him on.

"Madame insisted they leave. I told her you were coming, Po, maybe she would want to stay and tell you hello. I know she likes you and I thought it might calm her down. I did not want her leaving my restaurant upset. The professor agreed with me. But she wouldn't stay—just grabbed his arm and repeated that she wanted to leave. It wasn't working out as she planned, she said."

"Working out?" Po frowned.

Jacques shrugged. "Professor Fellers told me not to worry. He said he would take her home and make sure she was okay. But before she left, she did tell me she liked my escargots." Jacques beamed. "She usually does not pay compliments, *non?*"

Po smiled. No, Adele didn't used to be gracious in that way. But Adele was making progress, and not just in walking on a swollen ankle.

"But," Jacques continued, pleased with such an attentive audience, "I think with Monsieur Adler in jail, people might begin to feel better."

"But disturbing the peace isn't the same as murder," Po said.

"Non, you are right, Po. But where there is such horrible anger, who knows what more the gendarmes will find?" Jacques gave their order for escargots and a ragout d'agneau to a waitress hovering nearby, assuring them it would please even his own dear deceased mother, were she here to try it. And before they could comment, he scurried off to welcome a group of diners settling in at a nearby table.

"I almost wish Jacques was right about Tom Adler," Po said.

"But he's not," Eleanor added. "Tom Adler is a fool, but not a murderer."

"But he's a desperate fool. Desperation can lead a man to do unexpected things. His wife is a demanding one, that I've seen close up." Max hailed the sommelier and ordered a bottle of white wine.

"Do you really think Tom could be responsible?"

"Po, greed and love are a volatile mix."

"That would explain Ollie's murder, maybe, if he thought he could really get the house if Ollie died. But not Joe."

"Maybe Joe knew something? Maybe witnessed the murder or saw Tom leaving the house that night," Eleanor offered. "And hurting Adele's dog and the fire might have been scare tactics to get Adele to give up her plan for the bed and breakfast."

The waiter silently uncorked a bottle of full-bodied grenache and offered the glass to Max to taste.

"Wonderful," Max assured him, swirling and sniffing the crisp French wine.

"I agree—it all seems plausible," Po said.

"But doesn't settle nicely in the heart, right?" Max looked over at Eleanor and lifted his glass in the air. "To the birthday girl," he said.

They clinked their glasses together.

"Happy birthday, dear Eleanor." Po sipped her wine and smiled at her friend of so many years that she could no longer keep track.

And with the warm sentiments of birthday and friendship, and the delicious aroma of garlic and butter swirling up from the escargots the waiter placed in front of them, the small group moved on to more appropriate conversation, like Eleanor's planned trip to the south of France.

Later, when they were stuffed full of Jacques's wine-flavored lamb stew and slices of baba au rhum made especially for Eleanor's birthday, the threesome left the restaurant and walked slowly down Elderberry Road. Po linked her arms through Max's and Eleanor's and tilted her head back to look up at the night sky. It was black and beautiful, filled with a sparkling wash of constellations and galaxies. "Amazing," she murmured, her thoughts turning automatically to Oliver Harrington. He was never far from her thoughts these days, and she wondered when he would release his hold on her. When the murderer is found, her mind answered back. That's when. Po sorted through her thoughts, trying to untangle the threads and wishing the unsettling thoughts would leave her, move on, and let her be. She kept returning to Joe's tiny apartment, the life he lived there. And the awareness that the Harrington estate was his whole world. One he rarely left. Except through death. Who could have wanted him dead, a man who had no connections? A niggling feeling, a thought that hadn't yet formed, had been buzzing around her like a pesky insect. Since...since when? Since she left Joe's apartment?

Po looked up into the brightly lit window of Gus's bookstore. They walked over, looking in and examining his new display.

"I think I'll see what new travel books Gus has gotten in," Eleanor said, pointing her cane at several guide books featured in the window.

Max held the door and Po followed Eleanor inside the store, grappling with the irritating thought that dangled like a thread right in front of her.

The store was crowded, some people passing the time while they waited for a table at Jacques's, others wandering through the store, listening to a guitarist playing in a reading room, and others checking out the best sellers on a display rack.

Po spotted the owner standing to the side, talking to a customer. She wandered over to say hello just as the customer turned around.

"Jed!" she said. "What are you doing here?"

Jed turned and smiled. "Talking to Gus?"

"Shame on me," Po said. "That was rude. I'm not accustomed to questioning friends' whereabouts. It's just that we were talking about you with Jacques. He mentioned the unfortunate encounter at his restaurant tonight."

Jed shoved his hands in his pockets. "It wasn't pretty, that's for sure. Adele isn't the most gracious person in town, but Adler's behavior was pretty bad. I don't know what the guy was thinking. Too much wine, I guess."

"In spite of that, it was nice of you to take her out, though. I'm sure she appreciated it."

"Out?" Jed started to answer, then held his silence.

"Well, Adele gets what she wants, don't you know?" Gus said, stepping into the conversation.

"What does that mean, Gus?" Po asked.

"Not that there's anything wrong with women asking men out, Po. My Rita says it's done all the time with the college crowd and makes good sense."

"Gus, sometimes you talk too much," Jed said jokingly.

"Not at all," Gus retorted. "Everyone in the store heard her invite you to take her to dinner." Gus looked around, then lowered his voice. "And just between us and the doorknob, we were all pretty relieved it was you she asked out and not any of us."

"I ask Max to take me out all the time," Po said. "You're just too old-fashioned, Gus." She smiled at the two men. The news that Adele had initiated the dinner brought an unexpected feeling of relief to Po, and she wasn't at all sure why. Perhaps it was the look on Halley's face when she saw Jed this morning. Seeing Jed with a woman Halley so disliked would surely have disturbed that smile.

"Adele was in an ornery mood by the time I got her home," Jed said. "I think she was wondering why she'd asked me in the first place. And frankly, I was wondering the same thing. She said she wanted to talk with me about something, but we never got that far. I was fine with making it a short evening, though. I'd promised Halley I'd stop by her place, but when I got there, she wasn't home. I checked out a couple places, then thought maybe I'd find her here. Bookstores and libraries seem to be her favorite places. Have any of you seen her?"

"Not tonight," Gus said, but before the words had settled in between them, Po spotted Halley coming in the front door.

Po waved to her over the heads of several customers. "Over here, Halley," she called out.

Halley waved back and wound her way to Po's side. When she spotted Jed, she stopped short.

"Hey, Halley," Jed said. "I've been looking for you."

But Halley brushed his hand from her arm and took a step back.

Po frowned. Halley's behavior had been so erratic today. Tonight she seemed agitated. Her cheeks were flushed and her eyes darted from Po to Jed, then back to Po. Angry eyes.

"Halley, are you all right?" Po asked quietly.

"I'm fine," Halley snapped. She looked at Jed again, a pinched look on her face.

"I got caught up in something, Halley," Jed said. "I'm sorry. Adele—"

"Don't," Halley interrupted. Her tone was sharp, accusing. "Don't talk about her to me."

"Halley," Jed tried again.

Halley held up one hand to stop his words. She looked at Po and opened her mouth as if to speak, then closed it, her lips pressed into a thin line.

Before Po could say anything to ease the moment, Halley turned and walked toward the door, her steps angry on the wooden floor.

Jed looked at Po, started to say something, and then instead, excused himself and hurried after Halley.

Po was surprised. This wasn't the gentle librarian she had gotten to know in recent days. Jealousy wasn't an emotion she'd have suspected would come easily to Halley. Nor disallowing an explanation that could so easily have eased the moment.

Max came up behind her. "What was that all about? Halley looked like she was about to kill someone."

Po shook her head and looked at Gus. "How did you read it, Gus? She was upset, that was for sure. Maybe Jed will calm her down. He seemed concerned."

"I don't know what gives. Halley is usually so quiet and pleasant. But that wasn't the Halley I know. Jed has a job on his hands, far as I could tell. You know what they say about a woman scorned—"

"But she wasn't scorned, Gus."

"You know that and I know that, but Halley sure doesn't."

"Jed will work it out. The man's a peacemaker," Max said.

"You're right. Sometimes all it takes is a good night's sleep. Which is what we all need. Now where in this jungle of books is Eleanor?"

By the time Max and Po found her, Eleanor had confiscated several new travel books and Gus was about to lock his doors.

"Nothing for you, Po?" Gus asked, sticking Eleanor's credit card in the machine. "It's a rare day you leave here empty-handed. How about a little support for the professor? These just came in. Haven't even shelved them yet." He pointed to a small stack of Jed's new book sitting next to the computer. "I think you'll like it."

Eleanor picked up the book and added it to her stack. "My treat," she said.

"Now out, my friends," Gus demanded, returning Eleanor's credit card and handing her the bag. "I need to get home to Rita or she'll wonder what I'm up to."

"And we've had enough of that sort of thing for one night," Max said. "Let's keep the peace at all costs."

Gus laughed. He held the door open, then locked it behind them.

Keep the peace, Po thought. But she felt anything but peaceful. And even the starry night and two dear friends beside her couldn't shake the feeling that peace was not the operative word tonight.

Chapter 24

Max dropped Eleanor off, then he and Po drove in comfortable silence the short distance to Po's home.

They drove slowly into the driveway, headlights beaming into the black night in front of them. "Is that Hoover?" Max asked, spotting movement to the side of the garage.

Po frowned, peering into the darkness. She was sure she'd left Hoover inside when Max picked her up. But as the car pulled to a stop, Hoover emerged from the shadows of the garage, his tail wagging. Before Po could take a step from the car, he was at her side.

"Hoover, what are you doing out here?" Po looked over at Max. "That's odd. But sometimes Peter—that nice fourteen year old who mows my lawn—comes over and takes him for a walk. Maybe he didn't latch the door tightly."

"This is crazy, Po. Will I ever convince you that your open-door policy isn't a great idea?" He got out and walked around the side of the car, his tone more serious than usual on the topic.

But Po only half listened to the familiar lecture about safety. She leaned down, scratching Hoover's ears, and thinking. She'd have to talk to Peter about this. Although Hoover wouldn't venture far, it would only take one squirrel to send him flying across the street—and he wouldn't stop and look both ways first. She glanced down the street. She'd give Peter a call in the morning.

Max walked Po to the side door, Hoover close behind, and held it open.

"I'd ask you in, Max, but I know you're as tired as I am."

Max nodded. "And I've an early appointment with a client tomorrow." He held her for a moment, then felt the nudge of Hoover's furry head between them. Max pulled apart, then kissed Po good night. "I think Hoover's tired, too. Who knows what adventures he had tonight. 'Night big fella." He scratched the dog's ears, then headed back to his car.

Po watched Max drive away, wondering how she had been so lucky to have, not one but two amazing men in her life. "And you're not so bad yourself," she said to Hoover, opening the back door and stepping into the low counter lights in the kitchen.

Hoover ran around her, then stopped short, barking loudly into the semi-dark house.

Po's heart began to beat wildly. Something didn't feel right; clearly, Hoover thought so, too.

Hoover raced through the family room and into the front hall, his golden coat flying in the breeze.

"Is someone there?" Po called out, then pulled her phone from the pocket of her coat, ready to dial 911.

From the front of the house, Hoover barked wildly. Po peered into the darkened front hallway, the phone clenched tightly in her hand, her finger just above the programmed key that would bring the police.

Hoover stood at the front door, his ears alert, his nose pressed against the glass. All was silent, save for the beating of her heart and Hoover's panting.

Po walked cautiously to the door and looked out into the dark night. The solid inner door was pushed wide open. Po stood at the glass storm door behind Hoover, peering out into the darkness. Nothing but the dark, starry night. But someone had been here. *Someone had been in her house.*

Po shuddered and rubbed her arms. The feeling of being assaulted, of someone invading her private space was as real and poignant as it would have been if she had encountered a trespasser face to face. Po walked through the house quickly, flicking on every switch until the house was ablaze in light and the beating of her heart had slowed.

The fear had dried Po's mouth and she poured a drink of water from the cooler, then stood by the kitchen table, looking around the large living area. Everything looked the same as when she had left the house hours earlier.

Beside her, Hoover began to sniff the floor, then sniffed his way back into the wood-paneled den near the front door.

Po followed slowly, wishing she had asked Max to come inside with her. She turned on the overhead light in the den. Scott's massive old desk was where it always was. But all around it were pieces of paper, tossed about in disarray. The desk drawers were open, and pads of Po's yellow paper had been pulled out and left on the floor beside the desk. Po pressed her hand against her heart and tried to calm the rising fear filling her chest.

The gold clock the college had given Scott on his tenth anniversary as president was still on the shelf. Her laptop computer was where she'd left it in the middle of the desk. A digital camera sat on a table and an iPad in easy view. Clearly whoever rummaged through her drawers was not out to steal electronics.

Po had brought the pictures salvaged from Joe's apartment upstairs and put them on the table in the den, ready to reframe and return to Adele. Several were on the floor, but as far as she could tell, they all seemed to be there, though rearranged and turned upside down. Po walked back through the hallway and into the family room and kitchen.

There were no signs of anyone being in that part of the house, except the door of the closet where she kept her quilting supplies was ajar. Back in the kitchen she spotted a slightly open drawer. She probably had done that herself. She'd been in a hurry when she left, and had been preoccupied about the stash of things in her basement. She glanced over at the counter where she'd tossed the yellow pad she had been doodling on that afternoon.

It wasn't there.

Po frowned. She retraced her steps to the den, then returned to the kitchen. She had had the pad of paper in her hand, she remembered, and then had set it down carelessly on the counter and gone upstairs to shower and dress. She was sure of that. Because she had planned to go into the basement, but ran out of time.

The basement.

Po walked through the back hallway and down the stairs. She flicked the switch and flooded the basement room with light. The remnants of Joe's life were there, still lined up drying, their pages curled from the process. Nothing seemed to be disturbed.

The trespasser hadn't been in the basement. But a newcomer to her house would need time to find the basement. The door was at the end of a back hallway and she always closed it. Especially now, while the unpleasant odor of burnt paper still lingered in the room. Perhaps the intruder had been scared off before he got that far. Or maybe he didn't care about the basement. What was in basements—trunks and old furniture? Probably not a robber's treasure trove. She picked up a small, heat-singed book that she had forgotten the day before and carried it upstairs with her to put with things Halley might want.

Po refilled her water glass and sat on the couch, forcing her heartbeat to slow. Finally, with Hoover curled up in a golden heap on his bed beside the couch, Po walked through the house and locked her doors for the first time since she could remember.

She poured herself a glass of wine and carried it upstairs. She considered calling the police, but there didn't seem to be anything missing. What could they do? Instead she picked up the new book Eleanor had bought for her and headed upstairs to bed.

A soak in a hot bath, the glass of wine, and a few chapters of the book relaxed her weary body, and when Po turned out the light a short while later, sleep, though fitful, finally came.

Chapter 25

"Po, I can't believe you didn't call the police," Selma said. Her eyes were blazing.

Po had considered skipping the Saturday morning quilting session, but they were all nearly finished with their quilt tops for the bed and breakfast, and Po knew her absence would cause more fuss than sharing her news about last night's break-in. Now she wasn't so sure.

"Calm down. Nothing was taken. Everything is fine."

"Fine, my foot." Selma walked around the end of the table and plugged in the iron. Her brown clogs pounded on the hardwood floor.

"Have you talked to P.J.?" Kate asked, her face troubled.

Po saw the worry fill Kate's enormous brown eyes. She reached over and patted her hand. "Kate, don't worry about this. Please. I will be careful."

Kate didn't answer. She slipped her hand away and walked over to the sideboard, pouring a cup of coffee and looking out into the morning, worry visible in the sloop of her shoulders.

Eleanor lowered her cane to the floor and sat down next to Po. "Drink this," she said, handing Po a cup of coffee.

"Eleanor, I'm fine."

"Well, I'm not," Eleanor said, "so humor me. If I had my flask, I'd spike it."

Phoebe echoed Eleanor's concern. "Po, it's like this time it wasn't dangerous, but next time? We need to figure this out, stop all this nonsense. Why would anyone want to break into your house?"

"That's the first question that needs an answer. You said nothing was taken?" Selma said. "Doesn't make sense."

"Nothing, except for a yellow pad," Po said. "And most likely I misplaced that. I doubt if anyone would want my scribblings and grocery lists. There's even a chance I have blown this out of proportion and it was Hoover who scattered the papers in the den. Maybe chasing a mouse."

But even Po wasn't buying her own explanation.

"So is that what was on the yellow pad?" Maggie asked. "Grocery lists?" Her Fox and Geese quilt top was almost finished and she was as proud of it as she was of her veterinary clinic. She'd pieced the simple design with bright red calico pieces and it would be perfect on the double bed in the corner room at 210 Kingfish Drive.

"That and nonsense. Doodles, scribbles."

Leah and Susan walked in from the other room, carrying their already completed quilts. Leah had quilted her own, not trusting it to a second party. The spirit that comes with the presence of beautiful things filtered into the room, relieving the tension.

"That's gorgeous," Maggie exclaimed as she spied the quilt in Leah's arms. She got up and took one corner of the quilt from Leah. Together they held it high for the others to see.

For the quilt top, Leah had created her own design, piecing together a bed of rolling hills—strips of bright greens and blues, shades of rust and goldenrod filled the quilt top in uneven waves. And on top of the design, in crimson and yellows and purples, she had appliquéd sunflowers and daisies and black cherry coleus. Brilliant zinnias, their heads full and flowering. Between the appliquéd prairie flowers, she'd woven strands of prairie grasses into the design. It was a contemporary prairie flowerbed, a work of art, and quilted in graceful waves that matched the field—intricate, perfect lines of stitching. For the binding that held the three layers of the quilt together, Leah had found a navy blue fabric, filled with tiny dots of color that matched the flowers.

"Magnificent, Leah. You've outdone yourself," Po said, grateful for the shift in conversation.

"It's going in that large bedroom with the sitting room off to the side," Leah said.

A rattling at the back door broke into the conversation, and Po stiffened, then looked over at P.J.'s lanky frame filling the doorway.

"H'lo ladies," he said with a lopsided grin, not totally comfortable in a roomful of needles and strange tools he didn't understand. He walked over to the sideboard, helping himself to a cinnamon roll.

"Are you taking up quilting?" Po asked, wondering when Kate had managed to send him an S.O.S. text without Po seeing it.

"Not today, Po." P.J. walked over to her and bent low, his face not far from hers. "Heard you had a visitor last night."

"I guess I did, P.J." Po said. "But he didn't do any damage—"

"He?" P.J. pulled up a chair and straddled it from behind.

"He. She. I don't know the sex, P.J., but whoever it was saw fit to leave without saying hello. Nothing was taken."

"Except your peace of mind," Kate said from the other side of the table.

"Yes, that was shaken."

"Any idea who would have come in like that? Or what they wanted?" P.J. asked.

Po had thought of that question since five that morning when she'd pulled on faded sweat pants and a hoodie, and run slowly through the neighborhood, circled around the campus, and finally walked briskly all the way down to the river park and back. Who, indeed? She almost wished a camera or computer was missing. That would make it simple. An honest-to-goodness robbery. But as far as she knew, nothing was missing. So it had to be something else. Someone who wanted something she had—and couldn't find it.

"Po?" P.J. said. "If all those thoughts rattling around in your head were said out loud, I'd be a giant step further in understanding what went on last night."

Po shook her head. "No, I don't think you would be. It doesn't make any sense at all." But she knew deep down that it *did* make sense, it all made sense somehow—if only her mind could order it correctly. Was it someone she knew? That thought caused the deepest unrest. She could account for those she was with last night, but that was a short list of two. Her emotions fought any possible list she tried to put together. But the truth was, someone had entered house while she was gone. In those few hours, protected by her absence, someone had rifled through her things. Po rubbed her hands up and down her arms and sighed.

Kate bit down on her bottom lip as she listened to the talk around her. Po glanced at the emotion clouding her face and could read her thoughts. She was as sure as Po herself was that whatever happened at Po's last night was connected to the murders. And that thought caused ripples of fear to travel up both their spines.

P.J. saw it too. He walked over and looped an arm around Kate's shoulders, pulling her close. "It's okay, Katie," he whispered into her hair. "We won't let anything happen to Po. If someone had intended to do her harm, they would have come when she was home." And then he looked around at the room filled with women who'd inched their way into his life—Eleanor and Selma with their plain wisdom and humor, the irrepressible Phoebe and quiet, talented Susan. Beautiful, earthy Leah, And down-to-earth Maggie, smart as a whip, with a heart as big as Kansas. They were strong, independent women, every single one of them. And that was exactly what tugged at his emotions and caused stabs of concern to settle uncomfortably inside him. There was nothing those ladies wouldn't do for one another. Even if it meant putting themselves in the middle of a murder investigation. Even if it meant attacking danger head on and worrying about the consequences later.

Chapter 26

P.J. left the shop with worry in his eyes and creases in his forehead. He started to say something to Kate when she walked him to the door, but she quickly silenced him with two fingers pressed to his lips.

"We aren't foolish, P.J.," she said.

But when she returned to the workroom, the conversation had grown animated and emotional. Impatience caused voices to rise, and two hours later, when they had all gathered their supplies and readied to leave, a consensus was clear and voiced loudest by Eleanor, her cane rapping the floor:

"There is no way on God's earth that a regular old thief would wander into Po's home, then decide to leave without taking things. This is connected to Ollie's and Joe's murders, as sure as anything," Eleanor declared.

"And it must stop," Phoebe declared, punctuating the abrupt end of their morning session.

* * * *

Kate and Po walked out into a north wind that scuttled leaves across the road. Po shivered against the unexpected chill. "I'll drive you home, Kate," she said.

Kate nodded. She was shivering, too. But whether from the crisp, sharp air or the recent conversation, she couldn't be sure.

"El is right. We're all right. And surely Phoebe is right, too." Kate climbed into Po's CRV and snapped her seatbelt in place. "These deaths aren't about that house. Joe and Ollie knew or saw something someone didn't want them to know."

"I think so, too, Kate."

"So it's more personal, more intimate."

Po nodded. She pulled into the driveway of the small house that Kate's parents had left to their only child. It was a cozy bungalow, and Kate's parents had refinished it to its original shine, restoring the dark wood molding and filling it with midcentury modern furniture, clean and uncluttered. Po had spent many hours on the wide front porch with Liz, Kate's mom. Sitting, gossiping, comforting, enlightening. All the things best friends do. Sometimes they'd laugh about how safe their houses made them feel.

Safe. That's what homes should be.

"Are you listening to me, Po?" Kate asked, undoing her seat belt and shifting on the seat to stare at Po. "You're not hearing me."

Po forced a smile. "Of course I am. A little distracted I guess."

"Yeah, I guess." Kate paused, then said, "P.J. will pass everything along to those working on the case."

"I know that, Kate."

"And they will find whoever did this. Whoever did all of these awful things."

Po reached over and gave Kate a hug. "Yes," she said.

But neither spoke with conviction. The words were hollow. They both knew the police were working hard, and probably were uncovering things every day.

But it wasn't enough. Po felt more certain now than she ever had that there was something right in front of them, staring them in the face, that would put the pieces together.

And that thought tugged at her as she drove away from Kate's. One had to think outside the box, outside a house and a garage apartment. Outside a potential B&B.

One had to think of Ollie.

He'd been agitated that day. Upset about something. Halley had seen it. And Leah too.

From Kate's, Po drove directly to Canterbury University, hoping that the library would be very quiet on a Saturday afternoon. It was not a trip she wanted to make, but she needed to talk with Halley. Her behavior at the bookstore had been strange. And where was Halley before that, when someone was wandering around Po's house without an invitation?

Po parked her car and walked up the stairs to the massive stone library. When she walked through the turnstile, she decided that her luck was changing. Halley Peterson was standing behind the resource desk working on a computer.

She looks sad, Po thought, as she made her way around a book display. The range of emotions the woman had displayed in just a few days was remarkable. Joy, anger, jealousy, sadness. What would be next?

"Halley?" Po said.

Halley's head jerked up. Her face was drawn, and she seemed, at first, not to recognize Po.

Po waited for Halley to step in, to fill in some of the cavernous cracks.

Finally, Halley collected herself. "I'm rather busy, if you've come to see me." Her voice was formal and cool.

"We need to talk. Is everything all right, Halley?"

Halley managed a smile. "Of course."

"Did you get my message about the things I'd found at Joe's?"

Halley nodded. "Thank you. I came by last night—but you weren't home."

"And did you find it?"

Halley looked puzzled. "Find what?"

"The things you were looking for at Joe's apartment. The things I brought home."

"Of course not," Halley snapped. "Are you saying I went inside your house?"

"Friends do that all the time. P.J.'s been known to go in and eat all my leftovers." She smiled, trying to ease the tension between them.

"Maybe others do that. I wouldn't." Halley played with a strand of hair that had fallen across her cheek, twisting it into a spiral. She looked at Po, challenging her, her chest moving in and out as she tried to calm herself.

"Did you tell anyone else about Joe's things?" Po asked.

"Of course not. Why would anyone else care?"

"You're probably right. I haven't really gone through them. I've spread them out in my basement to dry and air out. But I'm going to look through them today—and you're welcome to see what's there. There's a photo of you and Ollie that you might like. Perhaps some other things."

Halley face was expressionless. She nodded.

An awkward silence fell into the space between them. "Well, then," Po said, "Perhaps I'll see you later." Halley nodded and looked down. Her fingers began frantically punching keys on the computer, dismissing Po. Her face was grim.

Po paused for a moment, then rummaged in her purse for her car keys. Her fingers touched the small book she had found at Joe's and dropped in her purse. Impulsively, she pulled it out and set it on the library counter.

"Here, Halley. Take this. It's from Joe's and perhaps belonged to Ollie." Then she forced a smile to her face, turned and walked out of the library, feeling Halley's eyes on her back as she walked through the wide front door. In the car Po tried to process Halley Peterson's behavior. Had she totally misread this young woman? Though Po had seen Halley's anger when she talked about Adele Harrington—and in Gus's bookstore more recently—the frosty façade she presented to Po today was something new. But if Halley was trying to rebuff Po, she was choosing the wrong tactic. If nothing else, her behavior only added to Po's resolve to talk with her.

Po's next stop was the Harrington mansion. She found Adele limping around in the back gardens, looking more relaxed, in spite of the still-swollen ankle that kept her pace slow and measured.

Adele looked up as Po approached. "It's nice to see you, Po. Is there something you need?"

"I thought I'd give you a quilt update." She fell in step beside her. "Susan and Leah have finished theirs, and the rest are nearly ready to go. I think you're going to love them."

"I've no doubt I will. I hired the best."

Po smiled. "I wanted you to know that I'm drying out some of Ollie's things that I found at Joe's. Some pictures. Some writings of his. He was very good, people tell me."

"Oh, I think I told you that. He was a lovely writer from an early age. I sent him a computer once—but he hated it. He said his fingers needed the feel of the pen in them, that his thoughts worked themselves down from his head, through his fingers and the pencil to paper. The computer messed up the route and his thoughts got lost." She spoke slowly, thoughtfully. Remembering.

Po laughed. "I thought that way once. I had to force myself to make friends with a laptop. And of course it became my *good* friend. But I understand what Ollie was saying. So he always wrote in longhand?"

"Always." Adele looked off toward the pond. "I found a bunch of yellow pads in his room, filled from top to bottom with his familiar scrawl. But I couldn't quite get myself to read them. The day I returned, right after Ollie died, I walked upstairs and found Joe in Ollie's room, sitting on his bed with the yellow pads on his lap, old glasses balanced on his nose. He'd been crying I could tell, but I was a mess, in shock, still trying to believe that my brother was gone. And this man I had never liked was in Ollie's room. I yelled at him to get out, but he refused to leave without Ollie's scribblings. Finally, I gave in. I didn't want them, not really. I just wanted Ollie back."

"Did he leave?"

Adele nodded. "It was odd, now that I think back. Joe was acting peculiar that day, muttering that it would be better for me if he had the yellow pads. But he was such a strange little man that I guess I didn't pay much attention. And I knew that I probably wouldn't understand Ollie's writings anyway."

Po listened carefully. "If I find anything in the things I've taken home, I will save them for you."

"Yes. Thank you. I've reached the point, I think, where I can talk to people who knew Ollie. For a while, it made me angry, that people like Joe and Halley Peterson and Jed Fellers knew Ollie better than I did. Even Tom Adler spent more time with him in recent months. And Ollie liked them all. I'm not so fond of some of them, but I've decided that keeping them at bay is foolish. I'm only hurting myself. They knew a part of Ollie I would like to know better. In fact, for starters, I want to build a small observatory here in Ollie's honor. I thought Jed Fellers would be a good person to talk to about it."

"That's a lovely idea, Adele. I imagine Jed thought so too."

"Well, my discussion with him was interrupted," Adele said. "We'll talk later, perhaps."

"That was your dinner at Jacques's?" Halley Peterson's jealousy was most definitely misplaced, Po thought.

"Yes. There are no secrets in this town, are there?"

"Jacques told us. He was concerned about Tom's behavior. And I am, too. You need to be careful, Adele."

"It was unnerving, but he was drunk, that's all. He's a harmless fool."

Po nodded. Adele was probably right. But she was wrong about one thing—there were plenty of secrets in this town. Perhaps dangerous ones.

"It will take more than a drunk to frighten me away. He has a demanding wife, that's all."

"But when people drink too much, you don't know what they're capable of."

"Some people are more dangerous when they're sober, Po. But don't worry. If I am anything, I am cautious."

"Adele," Po said suddenly, the question coming to her unexpectedly. "Why did you leave Crestwood the way you did, and not return?"

"I left for college," Adele said. It was a pat, no-nonsense answer, without the personal touch of their earlier conversation.

"But after that, when Ollie came home. When your mother died. You didn't seem to be around much. Perhaps I am treading on personal ground—please tell me if I am. But did you not get along with your mother?"

"Oh my, is that what people thought?" Adele sat down on a stone bench near a garden of mums and looked out over the yard. The sun was sinking in the west, dappled light painting patterns on wide stretches of lawn. Eerily peaceful, unnaturally quiet.

And Adele began to talk.

"I loved my mother, though we disagreed about many things. Ollie, mainly. She babied him too much. Protected him so severely because of his learning disabilities that when she got sick, she made Joe Bates promise to stay here forever because Ollie had never lived alone."

"Why didn't she want you to be that person?"

For a long time Adele didn't answer, but Po could see the years passing across her mind. Sadness and happiness, pain and joy. Finally she said, "It was my father whom I disliked. Intensely. He was not a good man, at least not in all respects. His affairs during mother's pregnancies—she lost three babies—were cruel, but when he bedded a friend of mine on a college break, then threatened me later if I said a word, it became too much. My mother urged me to leave this town and make a life for myself away from it all. She used to come and see me every chance she got—she was a good person. But she needed the money Walter Harrington provided. She needed it for Ollie.

"My father never cared for Ollie. 'Broken' was the word he used. I, the healthy twin, survived. Ollie was weakened. An accident, my father said, and he made it clear to me that I should have been the accident. Not Ollie. Not the boy.

"But Walter Harrington did genuinely worship my mother, in spite of all his transgressions. And when she laid down the rules, he complied, leaving her and Ollie to live their life as mother saw fit." Adele rose from the bench and began walking back toward the house. Po fell in beside her.

"We weren't exactly the all-American family, were we? But we survived. And I think my mother did the best she could. But even knowing that, I resented what this town, this house, stood for, for a long time. But when Ollie died, I decided I'd at least give it a try—try to make peace with some of the demons."

"I think you have," Po said. "Or are on your way."

"Not yet. Not completely. I still have that armor on, I guess. As long as there are still people out there who think I murdered my brother, I can never really fit in here, can I?"

The sad plea from the strong, implacable Adele Harrington touched Po in a way that made her shiver in the cool fall air. She pulled her wool sweater closed and buttoned it. "Adele," she said, touching her arm lightly, "Hang in a little bit longer. I think that will end soon."

And for better or worse, Po knew instinctively her words to be true.

Chapter 27

Po pulled out of Adele's driveway and headed home.

This time she wouldn't be distracted. She would go through every single piece of paper, every picture she had taken from Joe Bates's apartment. And she'd find the answers to all her questions. At the least, she'd get closer to the ties that bound Ollie Harrington to the few people he allowed in his life each day.

She thought back to her brief conversation with Adele. Why was Joe Bates so insistent that he get Ollie's musings? What had Ollie written that was so important to someone like Joe Bates, someone who didn't even like to read? Joe wasn't sentimental, that much she knew about him. But he loved Ollie Harrington like a son. And Ollie's murder had turned him into a mumbling old man, a man determined, maybe, to bring his murderer to light. That would have been Joe's goal. Of course it would.

And maybe he was getting close. Too close.

Po suddenly pulled over to the side of the road and found Gus Schuette's phone number on her cell. She tapped it in.

"Gus," she said quickly, knowing he probably had a store full of customers. "You mentioned recently that Joe Bates had come into your store shortly before he was killed. Joe wasn't much of a reader. What was he buying?"

As busy as his store was, Gus liked to chat, and Po waited patiently while he confirmed that Joe didn't seem to read much, but he sure loved Gus's garden magazines when he used to come in the store more often. But that day—Gus remembered it clearly, he said, because it was shortly after Ollie's murder, and Joe was a broken man. He'd shuffled into the store, made his purchase, and shuffled out, head down, face a mask of sad anger. He'd picked up a book Gus had ordered for him. Not a garden book at all. Gus didn't need to finish.

Po knew. It made sense now, what she should have figured out weeks ago. She hurried out of the store and drove home, scattering leaves on her driveway in all directions. Around her, night was settling in, the tiny solar lights like fireflies along the drive.

Po turned off the ignition and reached into the back seat for her purse. And then she remembered the box in the trunk. It had been with the rest of the things she'd gathered from Joe's burned-out apartment, but she'd forgotten to bring it in, then forgot it was there. A brilliant stroke of luck. She lifted it out of the trunk and carried it into the warm welcoming lights of her kitchen.

Po felt her phone vibrate and pulled it out of her pocket and saw the voice messages. She must have missed the call when she was at Adele's or Kate's. She set the box in the den, returned to the kitchen and held the phone to her ear.

The voice message on the other end was tight and controlled.

"Po, this is Halley Peterson. Perhaps you and I need to have a talk."

Po frowned. *No, not yet*, she said to herself.

She switched on more lights, then turned her radio to a Saturday jazz concert. The mellow strains of an old Miles Davis rendition of "Summertime" filled the room. Po found odd comfort in the clear trumpet sounds, but she knew it would take more than music to get rid of the chill in her bones. She needed Max, someone else in her home.

A quick call to his home went unanswered. Po started to call Kate, then quickly realized she didn't want Kate around right now, not tonight, and was relieved when she got voice mail. She left a mundane message and hung up.

Minutes later, with a large mug cradled in her hands and the sweet scents of orange and spices wafting up from the steaming tea, Po returned to the den and sat down behind Scott's big desk, lifting the lid off the cardboard box.

"Scott, help me here," she whispered. "Let's get this over with, however sad and distasteful a task it may be." She pulled out Ollie Harrington's yellow pads and began to read.

The pieces flowed together seamlessly, as they often did when the most obvious situations suddenly came into focus. The only questions remaining would have to come from someone else.

Po shoved the papers into an old portfolio of Scott's and snapped it shut. Another call to Max confirmed that he wasn't answering yet, and Po knew she couldn't wait any longer.

It needed to end tonight.

She returned to the kitchen and thumbed through her tattered book of numbers until she found the address. And then, with her heart in her throat, Po grabbed the portfolio, her purse and a jacket, and headed into the dark night. She paused briefly before climbing into her car and looked up into the sky. Millions of stars were flung across a deep velvet blanket. A perfect starry night.

Stay with me Ollie and Joe, she whispered. We'll make it right.

As Po drove down the street, she tried Max one more time. And then she remembered a late meeting he'd told her about. He'd stop by later for a nightcap, he had told her earlier. Po thought about waiting for him, then decided to forge ahead. The sooner she got all the answers, the better for everyone.

She punched the address into her phone and followed Siri's directions. She led her to a neighborhood just to the east of campus. It was a pleasant street, with modest houses and new condominiums mixed together. The address was in a small complex of town homes, and Po found 707 Elm Street easily enough. There was a light in the window, and Po sat in her car for a brief moment, then walked up the short walkway and rang the bell.

"Hello, Halley," she said.

* * * *

Kate finally reached Max as he was leaving his restaurant meeting. "Please come, Max. I got this kind of weird message from Po—and now she's not picking up." The frantic edge to Kate's voice startled Max. Before he could respond, Kate rushed on. "She asked me to bring pie to dinner tomorrow night."

"I don't get it, Kate."

"Max," Kate said, exasperated with the occasional slowness of such a smart man. "I've never made a piecrust in my life that didn't end up being used as a doorstop. Something's wrong."

Max didn't argue. Po had left him a message, too—she said to come over as soon as he could.

Kate was waiting at the curb when Max picked her up and in minutes they were in Po's kitchen. Hoover greeted them but Po was gone.

It was Kate who noticed the address book. And the only name on the open page was one they recognized. Halley Peterson.

* * * *

"Come in, Po," Halley said. Her face matched her white T-shirt except for red, bleary eyes.

Po followed Halley into the small living room and sat down across from her. "It's time you told me the truth, Halley."

Halley nodded, but when she began to talk, the tears started again. She grabbed a tissue from the nearly empty container and looked steadily at Po. "I don't know where to start, Po, but first you need to know I adored Ollie Harrington. Sincerely. He was my best friend."

Po had a response to that—that Halley had a peculiar way of expressing it—but she held her silence, waiting for the answers she was seeking.

"I didn't know what Joe had of Ollie's. Just some of his writings. And I knew he was a beautiful writer. He used to read things to me that he'd written.

"Jed thought if we got them back, maybe we could publish them, honoring Ollie in a special way. A book of essays, maybe. Jed said Adele would never do that. But wouldn't Ollie love it? And I knew he would. He always wanted to write a book. He was so gifted. He wrote like a poet. So I tried hard to get them, to do something decent for Ollie."

"You tried to break into Joe's apartment after he died—"

"Joe had told me he had Ollie's notes. He rescued them because he thought Adele would throw them out. And then that day—the day he died—Joe called me and said he needed to talk to me. That it was a matter of life and death. We planned to meet the next day."

"Why didn't you tell anyone?"

"I told Jed. And he understood. He knew Ollie was a great writer, he said. And that's when he told me his idea of publishing his essays, if only I could get them."

"And when you knew I had them—"

"I lied to you that day, Po. I was so upset. I loved him, you know."

"Jed?"

She nodded and the tears began to flow. "I told you I hadn't told anyone that you had cleaned out Joe's place. But I had."

"You told Jed."

She nodded. "Because I still thought...or wanted to think, that they were his essays that we would publish in Ollie's honor. But when I drove by that night, I saw Jed going into your house. I confronted him later and he said he was getting some keys he'd left in your kitchen. When you want desperately to believe someone, lies can be easily masked.

"But I guess I didn't trust him completely, and I was angry and sad. I was starting to feel used and I hated myself for it. And then you kept after me with questions. I just wanted everyone to leave me alone until I could figure out what to do."

"Did you know what Joe had of Ollie's? Did you know what the notes were?"

"Not at first." Halley looked up at Po and her eyes were filled with grief. "Just that they were Ollie's writings. Things from his classes." Her voice was ragged with tears.

"Po, Jed was the first love of my life. I'm thirty-six, and he was my first love. I didn't know what to do about that, don't you see?"

"I understand, Halley. Love can do all sorts of things to one."

"Jed wouldn't give me a copy of the book he had published, you know. He said he was embarrassed by his first effort, and really didn't want me to read it. I could read the next one, he said. I was so foolish. Even though I thought it was odd, I did what he asked. But when you left it with me the other day, I paged through it and knew what I guess I'd known for a while—I knew that I had heard those beautiful, lyrical words before. Ollie used to read the passages to me after he'd written them. I'd sit in wonder, imagining the stars he wrote about, the pathways and galaxies and amazing dimensions of the universe."

"So it was Ollie who wrote *A Plain Man's Guide to a Starry Night.*"

Po was talking more to herself than to Halley.

"Yes."

A loud noise behind them startled both of the women.

Halley spun around as Jed Fellers walked into the low light of her living room. He dropped Halley's house key on the table and walked over to where she stood, resting one hand on her arm.

"Halley, I love you. I'll explain all of this." He looked over at Po and asked her politely to sit down.

Po saw the bulge in Jed's coat pocket. She sat down on the edge of the couch. His voice was dangerously calm. He kept his hand on Halley's arm and continued, his eyes never leaving Po's face.

"It's too bad that you pursued this to such lengths, Po. We'd all be better off—you, me, Halley—if you had left it alone."

"But Ollie and Joe weren't left alone, Jed."

"I didn't want it to end like it did. I'm not a monster, Po." Jed half-smiled as he spoke, and Po felt chills run down her back.

"Ollie wrote those essays in my class, you know. Shared them all with me. They were brilliant, so I photocopied each one. All I had to do was add a transition here and there and a title. It all made a kind of logical sense to me. I was his mentor, after all.

"I called Ollie into my office when the publisher sent me a copy of the book," Jed continued calmly, "and I told him what a great thing it was—he was a published author, wasn't that great? I explained that it didn't matter whose name was on it, he was the vision behind it, and we'd celebrate together."

Beside him, Halley shook her head. "You're a fool, Jed Fellers. Ollie would never have agreed to that. I could have told you that."

"You're right about that. In his simple way, Ollie had a ridiculous sense of right and wrong. Black and white. He said it was dishonest. Against the law. He explained that he was going to go to the chancellor and tell him. I tried everything I could think of to change his mind. I needed that book publication, for God's sake. The tenure committee was breathing down my neck. The department chair was at stake. Ollie didn't need it. I did. When Ollie wouldn't cooperate, I had no choice."

"But to kill him?" Halley screamed at Jed and jerked her arm away.

Jed slapped her. "Calm down," he said. His voice was monotone now and Po recognized the lack of emotion, the distance, and it frightened her. "Po, you don't get it because you've always had it easy. You and Scott. You don't know what it's like."

Jed's tone was changing dramatically, and Po stiffened. "You killed a lovely man, Jed. And you stole from him."

"Not a theft, Po!" Jed's voice changed again. It was loud and threatening now. "Who do you think taught Oliver those things? Who?"

"I'm sure you taught him many things, Jed. But you also took his words and told people they were yours. Ollie must have told Joe Bates about it."

"Of course he did. And Joe would have done anything for Ollie. Joe took the original essays after Ollie died, I was sure of it. All written on yellow pads, just like everything he wrote. Everything he turned in to me."

"So you tried to burn his place down? It was you, not Halley."

Jed laughed. "Halley? Halley couldn't hurt a flea, but she'd do anything for a friend." His hand moved up to Halley's neck and he tugged lightly on a strand of her hair. "But when Halley couldn't get the notebooks, burning the place seemed the easiest way out."

"And now what?" Po turned to face him directly. She'd known Jed Fellers for over a dozen years. Or she thought she had. But suddenly, she was forced to face a man she didn't know at all. Jed stood straight and looked her in the eye. "I don't know, Po. What do you think we should do?" He shrugged and looked at her with total disinterest. "I thought I'd find the manuscripts before you did, and no one would ever have known. But you butted in. And I know one thing, I can't let you destroy my reputation." His hand slipped into his pocket.

Beside him, Halley rubbed her arms, then took a step away. A noise from the kitchen distracted Jed for the one brief moment that Halley needed, and while Po watched, she raised her knee, positioned her hand for a chop to his throat, and before Po could get up from the couch, she sent Jed Fellers flying to the floor.

In the next instant, Max appeared in the doorway, followed by the police. He wrapped his arm around Halley. "That was quite a move, young lady."

"I walk home alone from the library nearly every night. A girl has to be ready," she said, and moved over to Po, hugging her tightly.

Outside, lined up along the green lawn beneath a perfect, star-filled sky, stood a whole collection of Crestwood police, waiting eagerly for their prey.

And behind them, shivering beneath the folds of P.J.'s down jacket, Kate looked up beyond the stars and thanked her mother once again for looking out for those she loved.

Epilogue

You are cordially invited to
Thanksgiving Dinner
210 Kingfish Drive
RSVP—Adele Harrington

Adele had decided that Thanksgiving would be the perfect weekend to open the doors of 210 Kingfish Drive to the town that had finally embraced her as one of its own.

With a crew of many and the help of Jacques St. Pierre and his staff at the French Quarter, Adele threw a Thanksgiving dinner that would be remembered and talked about for a long, long time.

"Adele, you've definitely outdone yourself," Po said, walking through the wide welcoming front door with Eleanor and Max on either side of her. "It's absolutely beautiful!"

In the four weeks since the jail doors had banged closed on Jed Fellers, Adele Harrington had thrown herself full force into finishing the renovation of her home in time for the holiday. The knowledge that Ollie's murderer was a man she knew, a man who was so present during all their grieving, was difficult to accept, and work provided an appropriate antidote to the pain.

Dozens of mums in rusts and gold filled the warm, inviting entryway of the home. Candles warmed tabletops and the soft light of sconces welcomed guests into Crestwood's newest B&B.

Kate walked through the open door on P.J.'s arm. "I want to be married right here, in this amazing place. Can we do that, Adele?" She smiled over at their hostess.

Adele wrapped an arm around Kate and took her over to the staircase, just beyond the small desk where visitors would soon be signing in. "How proud I'd be to have little Kate Simpson be the first bride to come down those stairs. Adele pointed up the massive winding staircase that led to the second level. Thick forest-green carpet lined the stairs, and ropes of garlands lit with tiny white lights were wound around the walnut railing. A harvest tree decorated the landing.

"I guess I'll have to find a man first," Kate laughed.

"Oh, they're all over the place. A dime a dozen," Adele said, a new kind of smile softening her face. The looseness she was feeling was rejuvenating.

"Hey, what did I miss?" P.J. said, following the two women. "Wedding? Katie, am I invited?"

Po watched P.J. follow Kate up the stairs to tour the renovated bedroom suites. A wedding at 210 Kingfish Drive? The thought filled her with a rush of dizzying warmth.

"You're wearing your heart on your lovely sleeve, Po," Max whispered in her ear, then handed her a crystal glass of punch.

Po chuckled and walked on into the spacious living room where Selma and Susan were sitting on a couch in front of the blazing fire. Gus and Rita Schuette were off to the side, admiring the built-in bar that Adele would use for evening wine tastings, and the mayor and college chancellor sat watching a football game in a small alcove area off the living room.

"Something for everyone," Po said, looking around.

"This place is amazing," Maggie said, coming up behind Po. "I'm crazy about it, and Adele has already promised me that we can have a fundraiser for the animal rescue league here."

Tim and Leah came in carrying Leah's homemade pumpkin pies, and Po helped Tim carry them back to the kitchen. "Jacques," she called out as they walked in, "here are more pies for your spread."

Jacques swooped over to them, kissing them both on each cheek and motioning toward the sideboard, where pumpkin and apple pies were already lined up.

"A feast fit for a French pilgrim," Jacques exclaimed with glee.

Halley appeared from the back room with Neptune the cat in her arms.

"Oh, I'm so glad you're here," Po said, giving her a warm hug.

"I guess you haven't heard, Po."

"What's that, dear?"

"Adele has hired me to organize the library that she'll have for the guests. It's going to be absolutely wonderful, and I'll work here when I'm not needed at the college. It's kind of a dream," she confessed. "I can pick the books I want, organize it, make it cozy and wonderful. I can't imagine our guests will ever want to leave. There's even a fireplace."

Our guests. Po knew that Adele and Halley had talked, but she didn't know the outcome had been so generous and forgiving on both their parts. They had each been hurt terribly by a man, and they had both loved another whom they couldn't bring back to life. They certainly had a framework for friendship. Po was pleased to see that it had already begun.

When Adele called them all into the living room a short while later, Po was prepared for a toast. What she wasn't prepared for was the announcement from the president of Canterbury University. "There will be a new printing of *A Plain Man's Guide to the Galaxy*," he said, "with our own Oliver Harrington's name on the cover."

Adele stood beside him, her eyes damp. She wiped the tears aside and took her place in front of the fireplace. "In addition to the book," she said, "there's something else we've decided to do in my brother's memory." She nodded toward P.J. and Max.

The two men walked in from the foyer, carrying a folded mound of fabric. With the quilters standing proudly by, they unfolded and held up a hanging that Susan and Leah had designed, and all the quilters had helped stitch together in these four short weeks.

A gift for Adele. A tribute to Ollie.

The background blocks of mottled midnight blue held a brilliant galaxy, created from small crimson and gold and deep orange-colored strips. The design was a swirl in all shades and hues. The swirl spread out against the deep background, bigger and bigger, flying upward, until the largest star of all—a brilliant blend of bright orange and yellow and white fabric filled the top of the quilt.

Ollie's starry sky.

While champagne glasses clinked around the room, Po edged in beside Kate and Max. She looped an arm in each of theirs, her heart about as full as she could ever remember it being. There was magic in the air tonight, and she suspected she wasn't the only one who felt it.

She hugged her goddaughter close and spoke softly. "A wedding, Kate? Is that what I heard you say? A wedding on a starry night...I think I could handle that just fine. Just fine, indeed."

Turn the page for a preview of the next Seaside Knitters Society mystery

HOW TO KNIT A MURDER
by
Sally Goldenbaum

A mysterious woman arrives in picturesque Sea Harbor, Massachusetts, and the Seaside Knitters welcome her into their cozy world of intricate patterns and colorful skeins. Unfortunately, nothing frays a warm introduction like cold-blooded murder...

Available now!

Chapter 1

"Great bones," Spencer Paxton III said. "And look at these amazing grounds. We could have an extravaganza for two hundred here easily."

Spencer didn't look at his wife while he talked. Instead his deep-set eyes traveled over the wide lawns, the low winding wall that defined the property, a small guest cottage nestled in a clump of woods to the side. He looked at the sturdy stone foundation and sides of the mansion, the dozens of long mullioned windows. His eyes went back and forth, up and down, hungrily combing every inch.

One of Sea Harbor's finest.

Bree leaned back and looked all the way to the top of the three-story seaside villa. The fading light of early evening fell on the gabled roof, throwing shadows across the lawn and the flagstone walkway. The ocean wasn't visible from where they stood, but the sound of crashing waves behind the house and the feel of salty air heralded its presence. She pulled her hoodie tight.

"It's enormous," she said. "Twenty families could live in this house." She thought of the three-bedroom house in which her parents had raised their family of six. She had loved every inch of it.

"Yeah. Huge is good. We'll fill it." Spence walked his fingers up and down her back. "Rugrats. Maybe we'll get us some. Who knows? Things can change."

Bree was silent. No, contrary to what her husband thought, some things wouldn't change. Ever.

"I called a Realtor last week," he said, still not looking at her. His eyes were checking out the visible details—quality of materials, walkways, the grounds.

"You called a Realtor?" She looked at him in surprise. "Why?"

"That's how you buy a house, babe. I went to school with this gal—way back when." He laughed. "Stella Palazola. She was an upperclassman, but flirted with me like crazy. She had this big crush on me. I ran into her at the Gull one night. She fell all over herself wanting to help me out." He stopped and pointed. "Look at that balcony up there, the wrought-iron work. Amazing."

"The house we're renting is fine, Spence. It has wonderful light. I'm comfortable there. You won't be here forever."

Now he looked directly at her, his gaze sharp. "In the middle of that old art colony? My dad would roll over in his grave. Shove my face in it. No more. Canary Cove is a place for hippies and starving artists. Those knitters you hang around with would fit in there. Not a Paxton."

Bree smiled as his comment took form. *Those knitters you hang around with—those plain people. Ordinary.*

Wise, wonderful Birdie, who could buy and sell all the Paxtons without a blink of an eye. Elegant Nell, who'd once single-handedly run a large Boston nonprofit. Smart, gorgeous Izzy, with her law degree tucked away in some drawer of her successful yarn shop. And clever, dark-haired Cass, owner of a lobster company. Attractive, sassy, and exuberant.

Spencer had no idea of whom he spoke. And that was fine with Bree. Instead she said, "The home on Canary Cove is cozy. I like it."

"Not for me, babe. Doesn't fit the plan."

The plan. She looked sideways and caught the familiar odd smile that lifted the edges of his mouth, the lift of one dark brow. The set of his strong chin and the face that her own mother had compared to her favorite soap opera star the first time she'd brought Spence home.

"My old man wanted to buy this house when I was a kid. Did I tell you that? He wasn't fast enough, not savvy enough, and he lost out to an old Italian. Anthony Bianchi. It's my turn, babe. And I'll get it. They're doing some work on it now, fixing a few things. And then it'll be mine."

And it would be his, Bree knew. *What Spencer Paxton wanted, Spencer Paxton got.* She started to turn back toward the street, scattering leaves with the toe of her boot.

"Hey, where're you going? I'm not ready to leave yet. Come on," Spence said. He nodded toward the walkway circling the house. "Let's look around back."

"That's trespassing."

Spence laughed, and cupped her elbow roughly, prodding her along the flagstone path toward the back of the house.

Bree shook off his hand and put distance between them. She peered through the thick windows as they walked, but she saw nothing inside. Heavy black curtains held the dark tightly inside. Closed shutters protected smaller windows above.

When they reached the back of the house, a blast of damp ocean air lifted Bree's platinum hair and whipped it across her cheeks, stinging her fair skin. She pulled it back with one hand, bunching it as she looked out at the ocean. The surf was just yards from where she stood, down a terraced lawn and a footpath to a sliver of beach. Dark waves leapt in the air, then crashed against a graveyard of granite boulders, foam spewing in all directions. A small boat, moored nearby, rolled with the motion, tossing and turning in the cold air.

She breathed it all in, the air cold and bracing, until she felt she would burst. The ocean was magnificent.

She felt Spence's presence next to her, tall and dark and self-assured, his body shadowing her own. He had raised his binoculars and was scanning the horizon, as if waiting for a whale to perform, a fleet of schooners to parade past him in homage, or, *Who knows,* Bree thought, *maybe to spot an island for sale?* He lifted one hand and pointed south.

"You can see the Boston skyline from here," he said. "It's incredible."

Bree had turned away and looked up at the mansion again, the glory of the ocean sucked out of her by the sight of the house. She walked back to the fan of steps leading to a stone patio that stretched the width of the mansion. Yellow, orange, and rose-colored leaves skittered across the stones. The veranda was wide and empty, save for groupings of chairs and tables covered in canvas—gray ghosts in the fading light.

Bree shivered, wrapping her arms tightly around herself, wondering about the power this house seemed to have over her, blurring the grandeur of the ocean and filling her instead with uncomfortable prickly feelings.

It was just a house. A formidable one, and grand, too. She would give Spencer that. A majestic fortress, But it was still a *house*. Nothing else. She shook her head, only half believing her words. A *house*, she repeated.

"I'm going back around to the front," she called out, her words tossed away by the wind.

Spence was halfway down the flat steps leading to the water.

It was a while later, after taking photos with his phone and walking the stone patio for dimensions and imagining the events he could host on the property, the people he could impress, that Spence walked back to the front of the estate. Bree was sitting on a low stone wall that bordered the property.

"Hey, what's with you?"

"I'm tired and it's freezing out here. It's time to leave. I promised Izzy and Nell I'd stop by the yarn shop to help with a window design. They'll be waiting for me." *And I like them,* she said silently. *I like their friendship and their yarn shop and the warm feeling I have when I sit in the back room and make magical things out of silk and cotton and bamboo.*

She stood and looked once more at the house, as if it might have been a trick of her imagination. But it was still there. She stared at the curtained windows and the foreboding stillness within.

The windows stared back.

Spence forked his fingers through his hair. "You're being weird tonight. Do you have PMS? Get a grip, Bree."

Bree didn't answer her husband. She took a deep breath and tried to shake the feeling that was chilling her bones. Slowly, she released it and braced herself, as if the house itself was about to reach out and grab her. Unconsciously she flexed the muscles in her arms, strong and toned and ready to ward off danger.

Spence looked over at her, then back at the house. "Do you want to look inside? Is that it?"

She looked at him. "Break in? Of course, the perfect way to endear you to Sea Harbor voters."

Spencer laughed. "I'm serious. Not about the breaking in, but I could make it happen."

Bree took a few steps away, then glanced at the house again as if it might follow her.

"Something's going on here," Spence said. "What is it?"

"Nothing. It's nothing." *But it isn't nothing. It's something. Or someone. Sometimes feelings become tangled and complicated, the reasons for them blurred. But whatever is worming its way through me is real, a warning that things aren't always what they seem to be.*

Without waiting for another question or reply or subtle rebuke, she walked through the gate, out to the safety of the sidewalk and the narrow winding road that ran in front of the stately Sea Harbor Cliffside homes.

Spence caught up with her as they reached the car. He started to say something, then thought better of it and clamped his mouth shut, holding in his irritation, and walked around the car, sliding in behind the wheel. Bree stood on the passenger side, her fingers curled tightly on the door handle, her body still and her eyes peering through the towering trees, back to the house that stood at the top of the incline, proud and haughty. Sure of itself.

She stood there for several more minutes, until an irritated tap of the horn pulled her attention away. But the house wasn't done with her and she looked back once more, meeting its glare, returning it with a silent vow:

I will never live in you, house. Never. Bad things will happen there.

Then she opened the door and climbed into the car, the engine already running and Spence's long fingers tapping impatiently on the steering wheel.

"It's perfect," he said to his wife, reaching over and patting her thigh. "Just perfect."

Chapter 2

Rose Chopra stood on the sidewalk, oblivious to the life teeming around her. Her palms were damp, her stomach tight. Behind her, fishing boats were making their way to the docks, ropes were thrown, rough voices shouted, and crates and traps opened and emptied. Scolding and big laughter carried on the wind.

It had taken her by surprise, the sensation that snaked its way through her body. Her shoulders stooped automatically, years of yoga gone in an instant.

And for that one brief moment, Rose Chopra wanted to shrink to nothing.

She was eleven years old, sitting in the stern of a sailboat. Her chin lowered to her chest, her body folding in on itself, disappearing. She prayed for the ocean to open its mouth and swallow her.

And then, as suddenly as the moment came, it passed. Gone. Poof. Disappeared. Pushed away in an instant.

Rose straightened up, shoulders back, and took a deep breath. Her shoulders shifted and fell into a comfortable place; her smile lifted to the sky. *Head over heart. Namaste.*

She took a step back from the curb as a freckled-faced boy flew by on a skateboard, his hair flying wildly and his grin proud and wide. Rose grinned back, feeling confidence fill her bones and her mind. She continued on down Harbor Road.

Parts of downtown Sea Harbor appeared untouched by the years. Sights and sounds were familiar: people heading home from work, fishmongers packaging up the day's catch. And the incessant caw of the gulls and blasts of the lobster boats' horns coming in after a long day. It was comfortable. Easy. Not foreboding.

She slowed as the familiar blend of garlic, olive oil, and tomato sauce assaulted her senses wondrously from Harry Garozzo's deli. She stopped and looked through the window. It was still there, the ratty, slightly sun-bleached sign in the window. SEA HARBOR'S ONLY TRUE MUFFULETTA, it read. *And the only one*, people joked.

But what Rose remembered best was that Harry offered half muffulettas—for delicate appetites, he said—but Rose always got the whole roll, stuffed with briny, garlicky vegetables and every kind of salami and cheese known to man. Fat and thick and dripping with flavor. And she always finished it and it always made her happy, even when she went home with a button on her jeans loosened, her shirt pulled awkwardly over it. She pressed one hand on her abdomen, along with a grimace of shame. Even her dad only ordered the half.

Harry's deli would be here forever, she thought. People like Harry Garozzo didn't die. Without even looking, she could imagine the talkative Italian baker inside, his apron stained, his voice loud and welcoming as if he were standing in front of her, handing her the hefty sandwich.

The idea of coming back to Sea Harbor had rolled around in her mind for a long time, but always back in shadowy corners. Her mother talked about it, wished for it. Their reasons different, but both compelling and real. And necessary.

Rose would twist and turn the idea around until reasons for not returning had been smoothed away, erased completely, and revisiting the seaside town had been a given. Something she had to do.

It was true that she wanted to see the beauty of Sea Harbor through her mother's eyes, to savor it in a way she never had. But the reason she needed to come back was to throw away fragments of the past that were no longer a part of Rose Woodley Chopra.

Her old therapist, and then friend, had weighed in heavily. Many times. "Do this," Patti had intoned. "You're one strong lady, Rose Chopra."

Rose knew she was strong. Strong and mighty her dad used to say, his way of complimenting her height, the extra pounds she'd carried then, her strong face. But that same physique, when wrapped around a painfully shy preteen, was described differently by others.

She had stayed quiet and let Patti go on listing reasons why Rose needed some time near the sea, time to remember the places and pockets of the small seaside town that were truly magical. The place her mother loved so much she composed poems about walking by the sea.

The sea and me,
Its healing rush.
Infinity in its caress.

She had tuned back in to her therapist just as Patti finished her list.

You promised your mother you'd take her back to the sea. A promise that carried her through chemo and injections and excruciating days.

And you promised yourself, too. To do it for you, Rose. Patti's soft voice was caring and loving, even when she asked, And what happened, Rosie? You waited too long. And she died.

Rose had felt the air being sucked out of the room.

And that's when she packed her suitcase and headed to Massachusetts.

Rose realized she was now a block past Harry's deli, standing still on the sidewalk again. Like a statue.

"What do you think?"

The voice wasn't Patti's and it was no longer inside her head. It came from near her elbow. Rose looked over.

The woman wasn't looking at her, but at a shop window a yard or two in front of them. Her hands were on her hips, her head cocked to one side.

Rose was about to ask the woman what she was talking about. And then she stopped, her eyes concentrating on the stranger who had just spoken to her. The woman was about her own age, no, younger maybe, but that was where the similarities stopped. She was exquisite, that perfect beauty that stared out at you from the cover of magazines. Unnatural. Unreal. The woman's looks made Rose feel naked—as if every one of her own imperfections was suddenly in bold relief as she stood near the stranger. She had an urge to turn and walk away.

It wasn't until the woman's expression turned to confusion that Rose realized she was staring at her.

"You don't like the window display?" the woman asked. Then, as the woman brushed a strand of platinum hair over one shoulder, Rose realized her first impression was wrong. This wasn't unnatural beauty. It was the opposite. Pure, natural. Unaffected. Not a spec of makeup. She wasn't tall like a model, but small, delicate looking, but her tight jeans showed muscles beneath. And her Harvard sweatshirt, the sleeves pushed up to her elbows, indicated the woman could probably hold her own. Rose wondered briefly if she even knew she was utterly stunning—or if she cared.

Rose pulled her eyes away and looked at the display window.

Her eyes widened. "Whoo," she said, lifting one hand to her chest. The sound was more a breath than a word, like the sound one made when seeing a famous museum piece for the first time. She stepped closer.

On the other side of the window was a cave, a hollowed-out shape made of something Rose couldn't identify. Papier-mâché, maybe? She had made some with her sister's kids last Christmas. But this wasn't a child's molded rabbit or bird or a tree ornament.

The cavern-like structure was filled with gravity-defying formations— and they were all made from silky strands of fiber: icy gray and blue yarns. Stalagmites and stalactites knit into slender shapes, some that seemed to grow up from the floor, others hanging, shimmering from the ceiling of the cave. Tiny lights hidden in the crevices lit the cavern's beauty.

Rose took off her sunglasses and looked more closely into the scene.

A movement on the floor of the display window pulled her eyes down to a calico cat, unfurling from a nap. It sat up and looked at Rose as if they'd met before.

Rose stared back. The cat tilted its head to one side, its green eyes keen and strangely insightful. *So,* it seemed to be saying, *you're here. Now what?* Rose shifted from one foot to the other. Finally she pulled away, embarrassed that she had almost answered the animal.

She turned to the woman, who was still standing next to her, waiting. "It's amazing. What is this place? Heaven?"

"Sort of. Yes," she said, a hint of a smile in her voice for the first time.

But her face was still, and Rose wondered if she was one of those models who was told not to smile, to keep the wrinkles away. Rose felt a reserve in the woman, or maybe, she supposed, it could be shyness, although why would someone who looked like she looked be shy?

The woman went on talking. "It's a great yarn shop. I'm surprised there are still people in Sea Harbor who don't know about it." She paused, then looked directly at Rose as if assessing her. Finally she reached out her hand. "Hi. I'm Bree McIntosh."

Rose took the outstretched hand, the woman's friendly gesture a nice surprise, one that lessened the distance Rose had imposed between them. "I'm Rose Chopra. Did you create this window? These absolutely gorgeous pieces of art?"

"It's nice you called it art. Some people might not see it that way. Yes, I helped. It's a group effort," she said. "I'm a disaster at knitting sweaters and mittens. But I love to turn yarn into art, twisting and turning, playing with colors. We're having a fiber art show over in the Canary Cove Art Colony, and the display is partly to advertise that. I'm glad you like it. Be sure you come to the show."

"I love it and I will if I'm still here. It's amazing. And so is the cat. Did you knit it, too?"

Bree laughed. "That's Purl. She's a love. The yarn shop mascot."

"So you work here?" Rose asked.

"I help out when they need me. I'm teaching a class for Izzy and doing some things over in the art colony, too. Art is my therapy. Well, therapy on top of therapy. I've had both."

Rose looked at her, for a minute surprised. But she shouldn't be. Therapy wasn't her private domain. But, even after her own years of therapy, it still surprised her when someone who looked perfect needed therapy, too.

"You should come to a class, Rose. They're fun." Her voice was warmer now, as if somehow Rose had passed a test and they were connected.

"Maybe I will," she said. "Is the shop new?"

"I don't think so—but I've only been in town a few months, so what do I know? Someone said it used to be a bait shack. Kids would sneak cigarettes and smoke behind the garbage cans near the seawall."

A bait shop. Rose remembered it now. An ugly, smelly place with cracked windows and peeling paint. Her mother had warned her never to go inside—the smell would never come out of her school clothes, not to mention the danger that might lurk behind the bins of unsavory wiggly things. And she remembered the boys in the back, too. The cool boys. Smoking and sometimes worse things.

She had heeded her mother's advice about the shack and instead sought the safe and quiet sanctuary of the bookstore next door. Rose glanced over, pleased to see it hadn't changed much at all. A new paint job, maybe, but the gold painted letters on the glass door were the same—SEA HARBOR BOOKSTORE—with its creaky hardwood floor and the nice couple who didn't mind Rose curling up in a chair for hours, a stack of books at her side and her shirt smudged from the chocolate-covered peanuts she'd pulled from her backpack.

She had loved that store. And the owner's son, too. Her first silly crush. Danny, the tall, lanky popular kid, lots older and wiser than Rose. One day when he was helping his dad he'd noticed her huddled over a book, and he'd glanced down and read the title out loud. She still remembered it—*Dandelion Wine.* "Hmm," he'd said. And then he said that he liked Ray Bradbury, too. When he walked on, Rose wondered if he had heard the pounding of her heart or knew that his words alone had elevated Ray Bradbury to the status of genius.

Beside her, Bree McIntosh was saying something as cars rushed by, horns honked, and late afternoon shoppers moved in and out of shops. But for a brief moment Rose's memory blocked out all the sounds.

Finally she shook it off and turned back to Bree, but the blonde woman had turned away and was moving off down the street.

A man, leaning against a fence just a short distance from the yarn shop, seemed to be watching her. She probably got that a lot, Rose thought.

She watched as the slender, gangly-looking man pushed off the fence as Bree drew close. He stood tall, his thick hair pulled back in a ponytail. Everything about the man looked rough and messy to Rose. Even the bright orange bicycle next to him. He lifted up his sunglasses and continued to watch the woman coming toward him, and for a brief moment, Rose wondered if Bree would be all right. Then she scolded herself. She was in Sea Harbor. Of course she'd be all right.

She shook away the thought and turned back to the yarn shop, surveying it more carefully. Fresh paint, a bright blue awning, windows that sparkled. Everything about it was welcoming, including the sign above the door. THE SEASIDE KNITTING STUDIO.

At that moment, the shop door opened and several women walked out, laughing and carrying canvas bags with identical yarn logos printed on the side. One of the women glanced over at Rose and smiled. About Rose's height but slightly broader in girth, the woman wore a bright yellow blouse, tied neatly at the neck with a small bow. She paused, then cocked her head and opened her mouth as if to say something.

Rose shifted uncomfortably beneath the woman's look. But then the woman closed her mouth and shook her head slightly, as if apologizing for her stare. She turned away, stepping off the curb and following her friends across the street, horns honking to hurry them along. Rose watched their reflections in the yarn shop window as they gathered on the opposite sidewalk, mouthing good-byes before scattering in different directions.

The woman in the yellow blouse pulled open a heavy glass door between McGlucken's Hardware Store and an ice cream shop and walked inside. It was a door Rose knew well. It led to creaky wooden steps, a musty hallway above, and small offices huddled above the shops.

Rose remembered climbing those steps every week, heading up to her orthodontist's office, where her mouth had been filled with wires. Unconsciously she put a finger to her lips. The teeth were straight now, but the procedure never quite pulled her front teeth together. It didn't matter, her mother said. Gladys Woodley could name—and frequently did—every movie star with the tiniest space between her teeth. It was distinctive, her mother told her. And Rose was distinctive and lovely, too.

A scratching on the window pulled her attention back to the calico cat, its mouth shaped into a meow. Waving at her, its small paws moving back and forth on the glass.

Rose leaned down and pressed her fingers to the window, mirroring the cat's paws.

Come in, the cat seemed to be saying.

Rose smiled at the cat. *Okay*, she said, and headed to the door.

About the Author

Sally Goldenbaum is the author of more than forty novels, most recently the Seaside Knitters Mystery Series, set in the fictional town of Sea Harbor, Massachusetts. Born in Manitowoc, Wisconsin, Sally now lives in Gloucester, Massachusetts, with her husband, Don. In addition to writing mysteries, Sally has taught philosophy, Latin, and creative writing, edited bioethics and veterinary healthcare journals, and worked in public television at WQED Pittsburgh (then home to *Mr. Rogers' Neighborhood*).

Visit her at www.sallygoldenbaum.com.

Printed in the United States
by Baker & Taylor Publisher Services